Joseph O Barrett

The Soldier Bird

Joseph O Barrett

The Soldier Bird

ISBN/EAN: 9783743657984

Printed in Europe, USA, Canada, Australia, Japan

Cover: Foto ©Andreas Hilbeck / pixelio.de

More available books at **www.hansebooks.com**

"OLD ABE."

IDENTIFICATION.

The picture opposite is the Veteran Eagle in one of his grave moods, as he stood on his "Centennial Perch." J. R. Stuart, an artist of Madison, taking observations of the bird as he is, accurately sketched it from a photograph by J. M. Fowler, of the same city. It was engraved with fine effect by the Chicago Engraving Company.

His Excellency, the Governor of Wisconsin, has thus courteously given the author his autographic identification of "Old Abe:"

"EXECUTIVE OFFICE, MADISON, WIS., February 8, 1876.

"I hereby certify that this picture is a correct likeness of 'Old Abe,' the live War Eagle, carried for three years by the Eighth Wisconsin Reg't in the War of the Rebellion."

H Ludington

Governor

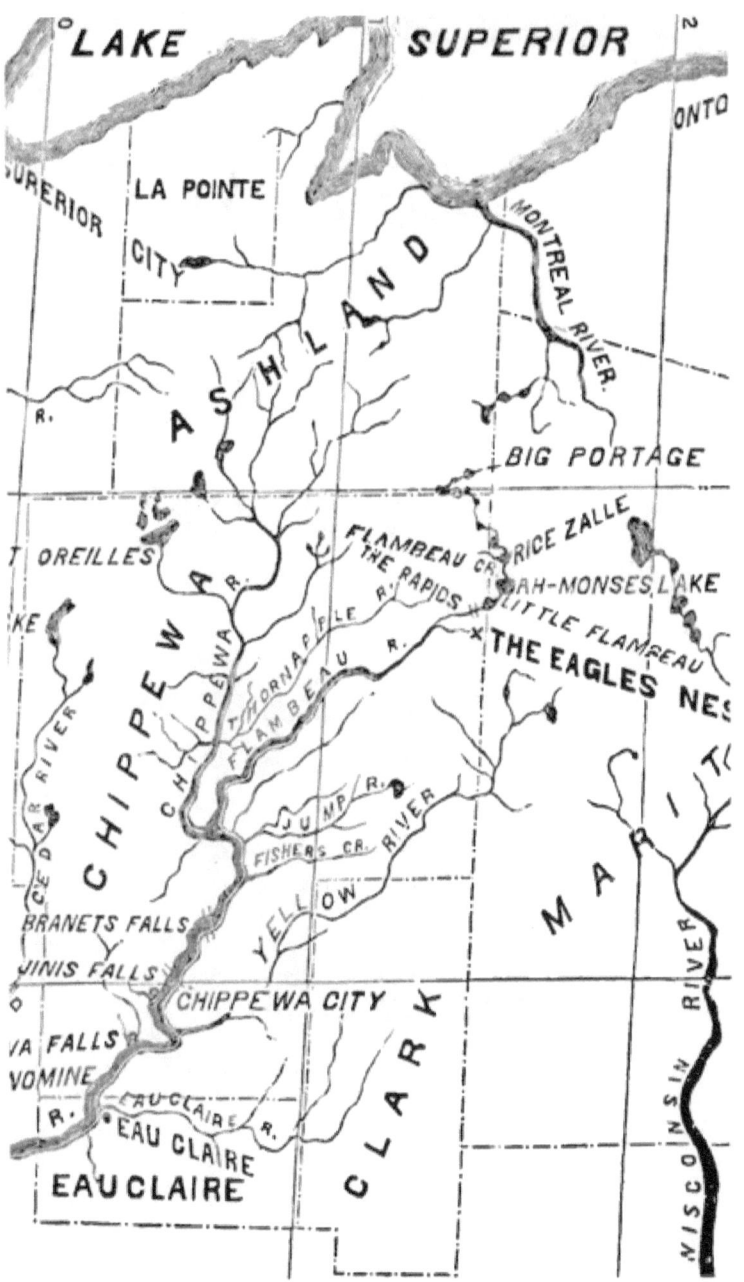

THE SOLDIER BIRD.

"OLD ABE:"

THE LIVE WAR-EAGLE OF WISCONSIN,

THAT SERVED A THREE YEARS' CAMPAIGN IN THE GREAT
REBELLION.

BY

J. O. BARRETT.

"When Freedom from her mountain height
　　Unfurl'd her standard to the air,
She tore the azure robe of night,
　　And set her stars of glory there.
　　　*　　　*　　　*　　　*
Then from his mansion in the sun
She called her eagle-bearer down,
And gave into his mighty hand
The symbol of her chosen land!"
　　　　　　　　　　　　— DRAKE.

"I'd rather capture 'Old Abe' than a whole brigade."
　　— GEN. STERLING PRICE, *of the Conf. Army.*

FIFTH EDITION.

MADISON, WIS.:
ATWOOD & CULVER, PUBLISHERS.
1876.

ATWOOD & CULVER,
Stereotypers and Printers,
MADISON, WIS.

TO

AMERICAN PATRIOTS;

WHO REVERENCE THE WISDOM AND VIRTUE OF

ABRAHAM LINCOLN,

THE MARTYRED PRESIDENT OF A BLEEDING COUNTRY.

TO

SOLDIERS OF THE FEDERAL ARMY;

WHO MADE THEMSELVES A BREASTWORK OF DEFENSE

FOR LIBERTY AND HOME.

TO

CONFEDERATES OF THE SOUTH;

WHO CHEER AGAIN THE EAGLE

THAT HOVERS AMONG

THIRTY-EIGHT STARS OF A UNITED REPUBLIC.

INDEX.

INTRODUCTION.

"AMONG all the incidents of this eventful war," says the Milwaukee *Home Journal*, of May 20, 1865, "few are more remarkable, than that an eagle, the emblem of our country, should follow a regiment through all the vicissitudes of a three years' service in the field." Such is the fact. With a view to the eventual publication of the biography of this celebrated Eagle, I undertook the task, while a resident of Eau Claire, Wis., in the winter of 1865, of identifying his Indian captor, that I might obtain a correct account of its infancy. The following letter from THEODORE COLEMAN, Editor of the Chippewa Falls *Union*, whom with W. W. BARRETT I had engaged to institute a personal research among the Chippewa tribes, explains the plan of operations so successfully executed:

CHIPPEWA FALLS, WISCONSIN, February 13, 1865.

J. O. BARRETT, ESQ. — *Dear Sir:* — Having been engaged for a short time in the collection of information relative to the capture and early ownership of the Eagle of the 8th Wisconsin Regiment, whose history you intend to publish, I take pleasure in submitting a few facts in regard to the progress made. Ascertaining, first, that the Eagle had been sold to Mr. DANIEL McCANN, of the town of Eagle Point, in this county, by some Indians, you wished me to discover if possible, who those Indians were, and to secure their presence at Eau Claire, at an early day. I learned from Mr. McCANN that the Indians who had brought the Eagle to him in the summer of 1861, were of the Lake Flambeau tribe, and that the owner was a son of AU-MONSE, chief of that tribe, or band, of Chippewa Indians. I proceeded to obtain corroborative evidence of this account, and found, through the evidence of Mr. JOHN BRUNET, Mr. JAS. ERMATINGER, Mr. CHARLES CORBINE, and others — all old residents of the upper Chippewa and Flambeau rivers — besides the testimony of different Indians, who were acquainted with the facts of the capture of the Eagle, that it was correct. All accounts agree that the name of the captor of the bird is A-GE-MAU-WE-GE-ZHIG, or Chief Sky, one of five sons of the said AU-MONSE. Having satisfied myself by such evidence, and by other inquiries made in every direction, that there could be no mistake in the identity of the captor of the Eagle, I have made arrangements, according to your directions, to bring the said A-GE-MAH-WE-GE-ZHIG to Eau Claire, as soon as possible. He is now with his band, hunting between the head waters of the Yellow and Flambeau rivers, and is shortly expected at Brunet's Falls, on the Chippewa.

Wishing you full success in the publication of your work,

I remain, with much respect, Yours Truly,

THEODORE COLEMAN.

Ascertaining that A-GE-MAH-WE-GE-ZHIG, with other hunters would soon arrive at Brunet's Falls, on their way up the river, Mr. COLEMAN engaged Mr. BRUNET to detain him there until a concerted movement. At length they came, *the* Indian with them, to whom was communicated the wishes of the "white man at Eau Claire," who desired to talk with him "about the Eagle he caught a few years ago." He hesitated, apprehensive of a trick, for all white men had not been true to their red brethren. Finally he appealed to his father. It was a grave question indeed; they were all afraid of being arrested for capturing an eagle! After a long counsel together, the old chief resolved to go to Chippewa Falls, without further waiting, requiring his boys to follow the next day, and appear in proper costume, should he find it safe. Arriving there, he had an interview with H. S. ALLEN, Esq., a pioneer resident, who, being a friend of the Indians, persuaded him to venture. Meeting his boys, as before arranged, he selected two of them, A-GE-MAH-WE-GE-ZHIG and A-ZHA-WASH-CO-GE-ZHIG, and with Messrs. COLEMAN and BARRETT and ELIJAH ERMATINGER for interpreter, rode to Eau Claire, the 19th of Feb. 1865, welcomed with a cordiality that at once inspired mutual confidence. The native nobility of these sons of the northern forests created quite a sensation. A-GE-MAH-GE-WE-ZHIG related his eagle adventures in a very intelligent manner, so simple and candid as to assure every one present of their truthfulness. His father, who is much beloved as chief of the tribe, was particularly loquacious and is properly named AH-MONSE, the "*Thunder of Bees.*" He had much to say about his "Great Father LINCOLN," whom he had visited several times at Washington, in the interest of his tribe, averring that Mr. LINCOLN gave him "plenty of money, and to his children much land, and let him see a battle field." Photographs of these "red brothers" were taken by A. J. DEVOR, of Eau Claire, and never did mortal appear more proud than the eagle captor when attiring himself in regal costume for his *carte de visite.* A full blooded Indian of consequence — then about twenty-five years old — belonging to the royal family of the Flambeaux, it is glory enough for him to be known among his fellows as the captor of the American Eagle of the Eight Wisconsin Regiment of Volunteers.

The following letter, with a map, gives an accurate description of the infant home of the Eagle:

CHIPPEWA FALLS, WISCONSIN, February 25, 1865.

MY DEAR BROTHER: — According to your request, I will give you what information I have obtained of the Chippewa country, and especially of the home of your Pet Eagle. Inclosed I send you a map of this country, being a perfect copy from J. I. LLOYD's New Map of the United States, with a slight change in the location of the Flambeau Lakes and tributaries, which are copied from a drawing made for me by AH-MONSE and the Eagle-Indian. I can find no maps representing the United States' surveys of these lakes. To-day I saw ISRAEL GOULD, the Indian Interpreter, who rendered you so valuable assistance last summer on your Indian expedition. At my request he drew a map of the Flambeau and its lakes, and it agreed precisely with the drawing made by AH-MONSE and his son. Mr. GOULD is an intelligent Scotchman, and has lived with the Chippewa Indians for fifteen years. He has a good knowledge of Indian character and probably is one of the best of Indian Interpreters. At one time he lived one year at Flambeau Lake, or Ah-monse's Lake, as it is most generally called, trading with AH-MONSE and his tribe, and, consequently, he is well acquainted with their country. I have much confidence in his account of the location of these lakes; and as all the other Indian traders, and trappers, and AH-MONSE and the Eagle-Indian do agree with him, I believe you can rely upon my map as being *correct.* I will give his description of this country:

The whole Chippewa country is well watered with innumerable streams, swamps, lakes and rivers; its surface varies in hills and bluffs, prairies, oak openings and meadows, and is covered, for the most part, with every variety of hard wood, Norway and white pine. The soil in many places is good, while many of the hills and bluffs are rocky, and in its northern portion are to be found iron, copper and other minerals. It is inhabited by the various tribes of the Chippewa Indians, and abounds in wild beasts, fish and birds. The Flambeau River is a wide, crooked stream, the longest tributary of the Chippewa, and its general course is southwest. Upon its north fork are the 'Rapids,' at which place the Eagle-Indian said he caught the Eagle. It is about 125 miles from Eau Claire, 70 miles from the mouth of Flambeau River, and 80 or 90 miles from Lake Superior. It is three miles from here to

Little Flambeau, or Asken Lake, which is three miles long; six miles fur ther north is Flambeau, or Ah-mouse's Lake—a stream uniting the two. This is the largest of the Flambeau Lakes, being three miles wide and six long. It is a beautiful stream of clear, pure water, where are found fish of many varieties. The meaning of its Indian name is 'Fire-Hunting Lake.' Near its northern shore is a fine island, where AH-MONSE frequently lives. On its eastern shore is a pretty, sloping hill, nearly forty feet high, covered with maples. Here, overlooking the lake, the Indians, a few years ago, had their villages, which are now located upon the north and northwest shores, where they have cleared their land, leaving now and then a shade tree, giving the country a beautiful appearance. The soil is good; and here they raise their corn and potatoes. Farther to the north is Rice Lake, the chain of lakes, the Big Portage and the Montreal River. A few years ago, this was the route of the Indian traders, going from Lake Superior to Eau Claire. The country near the lakes, for two miles east and west of the river, and about four miles in all directions from the lakes, is low prairie land, covered with hard wood, with here and there a lonesome pine; while beyond, in all directions, the country is uneven and hilly, and wooded with the dark pine. In this sequestered country, AH-MONSE and his tribe have lived for many years, subsisting upon their corn and potatoes, rice and sugar, fish and game. The Flambeau tribe is the most enterprising and intelligent of the Chippewas. Their warriors number from 140 to 150 men, and they kill more game than any other tribe. Here are found the deer and elk, the mink and marten, the bear and otter, and also the fish-hawk, the owl, the eagle and other birds.

Mr. GOULD says the region of the Flambeau Lakes is an *eagle* country, he having seen more there than in any other, and has there found many eagles' nests, containing from two to four young birds. Having seen the War Eagle at different times, he is satisfied it is a *bald* eagle; and this is the opinion of A-GE-MAH-WE-GE-ZHIG. Mr. GOULD also says, Asken Lake is situated about five miles east of the fourth principal meridian, which line is well defined upon the river bank; and, if he is correct, and I rely upon his statement, then the Eagle must have been caught in *Chippewa County,* in or near township forty, north of range one, east of the fourth principal meridian, nearly four miles from its eastern boundary.

Trusting my map and letter may aid you in obtaining a better idea of the home of the Eagle,

I remain, your brother, for Freedom and Union,

W. W. BARRETT.

By examining the map, the reader will notice the location of the birth-place of the Eagle that is now so famous in the world. His captor said the nest was found on a pine tree, about three miles from the mouth of the Flambeau, near some rapids in a curve of the river; that, at the proper time, just after sugar-making at the "bend," he and another Indian cut the tree down, and, amid the menaces of the parent birds, caught two young eaglets, of a greyish-brown color, about the size of prairie hens, one of which died from the effects of an injury; that they preserved the old nest — "big as a washtub, made of sticks, turf and weeds"— and nursed his *Me-kee-zeen-ee* (Little Eagle) in it, as a plaything for the pappooses at the Indian village; that, a few weeks after, while en route for Chippewa Falls and Eau Claire, with their furs, moccasins and baskets, he sold his Eagle to DANIEL MCCANN for a bushel of corn.

This statement of "Chief Sky" — quite a significant name — agrees with that of Mr. MCCANN, who subsequently tried to sell the bird to a company, then just forming at the Falls for the 1st Wisconsin Battery, but, failing, carried it to Eau Claire, some time in August, 1861, and offered it to a company organizing for the Eighth Wisconsin Infantry. It was then about two months old.

About the close of the war, being personally acquainted with some of the Eagle-Bearers and other members of the company, I obtained from them most of the facts herein related of the bird's "Southern life," dressed in their own apt language, which I have frequently used in this work, with their minute and graphic description of battle scenes. In writing up their and others' testimony, I have, of course, made the Eagle the central figure, not intending to furnish a complete delineation of the regimental movements, nor its official relations, but simply to mention instances where our hero acted some conspicuous part worthy of record. For many of these facts and incidents, I here acknowledge my indebtedness to Lieut. BURNETT DEMOREST, Capt. VICTOR WOLF, THOS. B. BUTLER, THEODORE COLEMAN, THOMAS and JOHN F. HILL, EDWARD HOMASTON, DAVID McLANE, Col. J. W. JEFFERSON, Serg't MYRON BRIGGS, DAVID NOBLE, GEO. W. DRIGGS, author of "Opening of the Mississippi," GEO. W. BAKER, HUGH LEWIS, Capt. ANGUS R. McDONALD, EUGENE BOWEN, WM. J. JONES, Mrs. G. P. HEWITT, Jr., O. W. GREEN, Mrs. M. IMOGENE GREEN, O. H. OLDROYD, Mrs. H. C. CROCKER, JOSEPH LAWTON, and W. W. BARRETT, especially, for his indefatigable efforts in procuring material for these pages.

With the testimonials of these friends and others, in military and civil relations, as vouchers for the accuracy of my history, I here respectfully submit it to the patriotic public, as an attractive episode of the Great Rebellion, appropriate to the Centennial of American Independence.

J. O. B.

GLEN BEULAH, WIS.,
Centennial Year, March, 1876.

"OLD ABE:"

THE LIVE WAR-EAGLE OF WISCONSIN.

CHAPTER I.

THE EAGLE A NATIONAL EMBLEM.

> What heroes from the *woodland* sprung,
> When, through the fresh awakened land,
> The thrilling cry of Freedom rung!   —BRYANT.

As the lion is king of beasts, so the eagle is king of birds. Homer calls it "the strong sovereign of the plumy race." Xenophon says: "The golden eagle, with extended wings, was the ensign of the Persian monarchs long before it was adopted by the Romans. It is probable the Persians borrowed the symbol from the Assyrians, on whose banners it waved till imperial Babylon bowed her head to the yoke of Cyrus."

The great banner of the tribe of Dan, borne by Prince Ahiezer, was of a bright green color, charged with an eagle as a component part of the cherubim, denoting wisdom and sublimity. The eagle was considered to be the symbol of Daniel, because he spoke with angels and received visions which relate to all time; of Christ, because of his divine nature; of John the Evangelist, because he soars to heaven in Revelations. The eagle was also the insignia of Egypt. The Etruscans are reputed to be the first who adopted the eagle as the symbol of royal honors, and bore its image as a standard at the head of their armies.

"The Romans adopted the eagle symbol at an early period of their history. At first, according to Dionysias, of Halicarnassus, they bound it to the scepter of their kings; afterwards, when they had toppled down the throne, they made it the ornament of the scepter of their warrior chiefs, and the only ensign of their legions. Under the republic, the Roman eagle was carved in wood; then in silver with a thunderbolt of gold in its talons. Cæsar was the first who had the whole cast in gold, but he deprived it of the thunderbolt on which it had hitherto rested. To mark his indefatigable activity, and his constant yearning after new conquests, the Romans always represented Cæsar's eagle with outstretched wings, as if seeking to enclose the entire world in the grasp of its shadow."

The eagle was the sacred bird of the Hindoos, and of the Greek Zeus. With the Scandinavians, it was the bird of wisdom, sitting on the boughs of the tree *uggrasill.* The double headed eagle was in use among the Byzantine Emperors, "to indicate," it is said, "their claims to the empire, both of the east and west." It was adopted in the 14th century by the German Emperors. The arms of Prussia were distinguished by the black eagle, and those of Poland by the white. Napoleon adopted it as the emblem of imperial France. It was not, however, represented in the heraldic style, but in its natural style, with the thunderbolts of Jupiter. It was discarded by the Bourbons, but was restored by the decree of Louis Napoleon, Jan. 1, 1852.

GREAT SEAL OF THE UNITED STATES.

At the time of the Declaration of Independence, July 4, 1776, Dr. Benjamin Franklin, John Adams and Thomas Jefferson were appointed by Congress a committee to prepare a device for a great seal of the United States of America. It underwent various modifications from year to year, until June 20, 1782, our present great seal was adopted. "It represents the escutcheon on the breast of the American eagle, holding in his dexter talon an olive branch, and in his sinister a bundle of thirteen arrows, and in his beak a scroll inscribed with this motto: E Pluribus Unum." The olive signifies peace, the arrows, war. In our flag, on which the eagle is sometimes inscribed, white signifies purity and innocence; red, hardness and valor; and blue, vigilance, perseverance and justice. "The escutcheon is borne on the breast of the American eagle without any other supporters, to denote that the United States of America ought to rely on their own virtue." Though Mr. Franklin was one of the original committee for the device thus modified and adopted, he pays the bald eagle a poor compliment when he fancied the turkey would be more appropriate as an emblem, because it is indigenous to America. In one of his letters he says:

"For my part, I wish the bald eagle had not been chosen as the representative of our country. He is a bird of bad moral character; he does not get his living honestly." After alluding to his tyranny over the hawk, he continues: "With all this injustice, he is never in good case, but, like those among men who live by robbing, he is generally poor; besides, he is a rank coward; the little king bird, not bigger than a sparrow, attacks him boldly and drives him out of the district. He is therefore by no means a proper emblem for the brave and civic inmates of America, who have driven all the king birds from our country, though exactly fit knights which the French call *chevaliers d'industrie.*"

How well the white headed eagle represents the Model Republic, let the incidents and facts herein related demonstrate. Our Eagle could tell Dr. Franklin how much there is in military discipline to develop the latent heroism of America, both in men and birds.

PETS OF SOLDIERS.

It is no uncommon thing for soldiers to take pet animals and birds to the war. In the Crimean campaign, the Russians carried cats on their knapsacks in all their marches and battles. Sometimes they rested on their masters' shoulders or heads, or hung dangling on their bayonets. They were frequently found dead on the battle-fields. During the whole campaign of General McClellan on the Peninsula, a Minnesota regiment had a half-grown bear which smelt powder in a dozen engagements, and was sent home in good condition. Several Wisconsin regiments had badgers. A rebel Arkansas regiment went into the fight at Shiloh with a wild cat, which was captured by the Federals, and afterwards killed by accident. Another Southern regiment had a pelican, thus representing in living form a symbol on the belt of Confederate soldiers. The 49th Illinois took to the war two game cocks of the first-class breed. Others had their heroic "Polanders" and "Shanghais." A Wisconsin drummer had a tame squirrel; it often danced to martial music, and spun like a top around the rim of its master's drum. The 12th Wisconsin Battery had a coon, which was taught many tricks, to while away the dull hours of camp life. The 102d Pennsylvania regiment had a large black-and-white dog, named "Jack," which was in about twenty battles of the Potomac army. At Malvern Hill, he was wounded. At Salem Heights, he was taken prisoner, and remained with his regiment six months on Belle Isle; and was also a prisoner for six hours at the battle of Middletown. "A brave soldier dog, intelligent and faithful, he was much prized by all the members of his regiment."

But, of all the pets of the Union regiments, the "Wisconsin Eagle" is the most popular, and his career the most remarkable and brilliant. He is a true American specimen, representing, in his actual bodily presence, the sublimated figure on our national escutcheon. When in good condition, his weight is ten and a half pounds. His breast is full and heavy, trembling with ardent emotions. His head is large, and well developed in front, towering up in moral aspect, and flattened a little toward the neck, where it is the widest. His beak, measuring two and three-quarter inches, bends in a semi-circle over the mandible, having its edges cut sharp, clear to the point, where it is hard as steel and of a beautiful flint color, but changing gradually toward the base into a sparkling saffron. The neck is short and thick, the body large and symmetrical; the wings are long and tail rounded; the legs a bright yellow, the tarsus three inches long, bare for the lower two-thirds,

2

and covered with hard, tough scales ; the foot short and full ; the toes free, tuburculous beneath ; the four curved talons on each foot have sharp ends, and look like grappling steel ; the thighs are remarkably thick, strong and muscular, covered with long feathers pointing backwards ; the conformation of the wings is admirably adapted for the support of so large a bird, measuring, from tip to tip, six feet and a half ; length of one, two feet on the greater quills, the longest primaries twenty inches, and upwards of one inch in circumference where they enter the skin ; the scapulars are very large and broad, spreading from the back to the wing to prevent the air from passing through. The plumage is compact and imbricated ; the feathers on the breast, back and top of the wings are a dark brown with a changeable gloss ; those on the head, neck and breast are narrow and pointed ; the other parts more rounded. The general color of the plumage is brown with a golden tinge ; the head and greater part of the neck and coverts are a fine snowy white ; the tail is also white, and spotted black on the upper feathers for about half their length; the quills are brownish black with lighter shafts. The eyes are clear and round, encircled with yellow papillary linings, fringed on their inside with thin, elastic, black bands or plates, like concentric rings; the iris is a brilliant straw color, and appears like the sky, changing in luster just as his moods are ; the pupil is large, intensely black and piercingly sharp, contracting and expanding with microscopic and telescopic action at every light and shade. When looking backward, his head appears in as natural position as when looking forward. The expression of his eyes is most fascinating; when inspired with ambition it is a burst of sunlight through a white cloud; when angry, every feather in ruffled rage, it is the lightning when the storm is on. He moves with grace and dignity, ever riveting the attention of the observer. Withal, he is majestic, having the intelligent air and heroism of a warrior grown bald in the service of his country.

ENLISTMENT AND DEPARTURE FOR THE WAR.

If peace can be emblemized by a dove — which Noah "sent forth to see if the waters were abated from off the face of the ground," the second time returning "unto him in the evening, and, lo! in her mouth was an olive leaf plucked off"— why not war by an eagle? Is not one as much a bird of heaven as the other? Among the significant devices of strategy and battle, drawn perhaps by unseen agencies in the solemn councils of the nation, where brave men and women appealed to the Lord of Hosts for protection, what more fitting than that an eagle, from the evergreen forests of the Great West, should descend from his eyrie to herald the march of armies in the morning of a revolution for freedom?

Though the emblem was thus strikingly illustrative of the hopes that hung upon the coming contest, there was some hesitancy about accepting it by the Eau Claire Volunteers; but through the sagacity and foresight of R. F. Wilson, an influential resident, who argued "nothing could be better chosen, not even the flag itself, to ensure fame and success," they looked upon it in favorable light, and after a surgeon-like examination of the eyes, claws, beak, wings and plumage, concluded by a jocose vote to accept " the new recruit from Chippewa." A little flurry ensued about contributions, when S. M. Jeffers, a civilian, purchased the bird for two dollars and a half, and presented it to the company. In due time the Eagle was sworn into the United States service by putting around his neck red, white and blue ribbons, and on his breast a rosette of the same colors. James McGinnis craved the privilege of superintending the eagle, to which all tacitly assented. In a few days he produced quite a respectable perch; and two patriotic ladies made some little flags to be carried on each side of him, when on the march; and gay and imposing indeed did he appear as he rode in imperial state beneath those miniature " stars and stripes," through the principal streets of Eau Claire, inspired by martial music and cheered by the enthusiastic people. The Eau Claire *Free Press*, of September 5, 1861, published the first newspaper notice of his honor:

" The Eau Claire Badgers are going into battle under the protective ægis of the veritable American Eagle. It was captured by the Indians of the Chippewa River, and purchased by the Badgers. Its perch is to be the flag-staff of the Stars and Stripes. Who could not fight under so glorious emblems?"

On the morning of the 6th of September, 1861, the merry drum beat the muster roll with unusual vigor in Eau Claire, and every volunteer answered to the call with an alacrity that betokened an earnest will. Some even danced as they stood in line; others, more thoughtful, were calm, appreciating the seriousness of the occasion, and just as resolute to depart for their country's battles.

"Forward!" shouted the Captain with emphasis, and on moved the company, led by martial music and the Eagle carried under the new made banner that had just before been presented by the women of the Ladies' Aid Society. It was a proud moment. What a sacrifice, what a strength of patriotism, what a price to pay for liberty, what a splendor of self-denial, when those fathers, mothers and sisters, crowding near, as if to assuage a soldier's anguish, said in every rainbowed tear, and look and prayer — "Go, my son!" "Go, my brother!" "my husband!" A cold drizzling rain beat down from the northwest, but scarcely was it noticed, so absorbed was the crowd in the intense feeling of the parting hour:

—— "Shout, sob, and greeting,
Love's deep devotion constantly meeting."

The company and people moved slowly to the levee on the Chippewa River, where lay the steamer " *Stella Whipple*." Held back by the entreaties of weeping friends, Capt. John E. Perkins found it difficult to get his men on board. What a strange commingling in association — the vast crowd standing in the rain, weepers many, soldiers resolute, and, on board the steamer, the Eagle lifted high on his perch by his Bearer, alone on the upper deck. He seemed a Roman soldier, while the Eagle, delighting in the storm and excitement, occasionally shook the wet from his pinions and flapped his wings, at which the little boys exclaimed, "See! the

Eagle is playing in the rain; he spattered drops right here; bully for the Eagle!" After much parleying and managing, there was a general movement of the volunteers toward the steamer. The bell rung, the engine sprung to duty, off swung the "*Stella Whipple*" in a graceful curve, and, just as she reached the current, three cheers from the people on the shore greeted that stalwart band, and hands, throwing kisses, and voices choked by tears, gave the patriotic "good by!"

Toward evening of the next day, when within hailing distance of La Crosse, Wisconsin, the steamer sent forth her semi-bugle notes, announcing arrival. In ten minutes the news was heralded through the city, that a "Company of soldiers from the Chippewa Valley has come with a live American Eagle!" Crowds lined the wharf, and, just as the boat landed, a salute from the 1st Wisconsin Battery, by order of Capt. Foster, was fired, followed by cheers from civilians and soldiers. All eyes were upon the Eagle, and deafening were the hurrahs in his favor. It was a thrilling enthusiasm of all that heaving mass of patriots. Capt. Perkins was here offered two hundred dollars for the Eagle. Quite a sudden rise in value from a bushel of corn. Courteously declining, the Captain replied, "The Eagle belongs to the company, and no money can buy him."

AUGURY OF SUCCESS.

Arriving at Madison, on the 9th, the company marched to a martial quick-step through the principal streets of the city, passing the Capitol, the colors and Eagle displayed in fine style. The reception was earnest. At

Camp Randall was a most inspiriting scene. As the company approached the hill, its musicians struck up the tune of "Yankee Doodle." The 7th Wisconsin and fractional parts of the 8th were there awaiting accessions; seeing the Eau Claire Badgers and their Eagle coming, they ran to the gate of entrance and opened right and left. During all this commotion, the majestic bird sat quietly on his perch ; but just as the company was passing the gate, defiling between those living rows of spectators, with a dart of his piercing eye to the flag floating close over his head, the Eagle seized one end of it within his beak, and spread his wings with a continuously flapping motion, expressive of inspirational ambition. It was spontaneous; the bird seemed to understand his mission, and grandly did he illustrate it as he proudly held the flag during the time of crossing the grounds, through the excited crowd, to the front of Col. R. C. Murphy's headquarters. A correspondent of the Eau Claire *Free Press* thus describes it :

"When the regiment marched into Camp Randall, the instant the men began to cheer, he spread his wings, and taking one of the small flags attached to his perch in his beak, he remained in that position until borne to the quarters of the late Col. Murphy."

The Madison *State Journal*, of the 10th, thus mentions the incident :

"An incident occurred yesterday, as the Chippewa company arrived at Camp Randall. They bore in advance of them a platform on which was a live eagle, surmounted by a small American flag. Just as they entered camp, the eagle expanded his wings and seized the flag in his beak. The incident attracted much attention, and if it had happened in other days, in a Roman camp, would have been regarded by the augurs as a singularly favorable omen."

NEW PERCH.

At Madison, the Eagle's visitors numbered thousands, and among them were dignitaries of civil and military professions. Here, by Capt. Perkins, he was donned with the title of "Old Abe," in honor of Abraham Lincoln, the faithful President and patriot. By vote of the company, the "Badgers" were to be styled the "Eau Claire Eagles," and, by voice of the people, the Eighth Wisconsin was designated as the "Eagle Regiment." As the Eagle was then a soldier bird, sworn into the service of his country, Quartermaster Francis L. Billings, at the expense of the State, had a new perch constructed. It was a shield in the shape of a heart, on which was inscribed the "stars and stripes," and along the base were legibly painted, "8th Reg. W. V." Raised a few inches above the shield was a grooved cross-piece for the Eagle's roost, and on each end of it were three arrows, pointing outwards, representing war as in the great seal of the United States. In the shuffle of war these were broken off. Evidently such a perch must have been a heavy weight for one soldier to carry, during the long and tiresome marches through the enemy's country ; but he had no other task than this, under strict orders to care faithfully for the bird. When in line, the Eagle rode always on the left of the color bearer, in the van of the regiment. In battle or march, the Eagle was carried in the same manner as the flag. The Bearer had a belt around him, to which was attached a socket to receive the end of the staff, which was about five feet long. Holding it firmly in his hand, the Bearer thus raised the Eagle high above his head, in plain sight of the column. A leathern ring was fastened to one of the Eagle's legs, to which was connected a strong hemp cord from sixteen to twenty feet long. When marching, or in an engagement, the surplus cord was wound around the arrow head, leaving the Eagle but about three feet length, or just enough to circumscribe him to his shield.

TRANSIT THROUGH CHICAGO.

On the 12th of October, 1861, the aggregate strength being nine hundred and ninety men, the regiment, under command of Col. Murphy, took its departure for the theater of war. As the long train of cars passed through the villages and cities of Wisconsin, great was the enthusiasm of the people; they poured forth rounds of cheers that fired every soldier with electric inspiration. At Janesville, the crowd was immense and intensely excited. It will be remembered that Rock county had given the first fruits of her patriotism to the country — company G, of the Eighth, led by Capt. Wm. B. Britton — hence the peculiar interest of the people on the occasion.

After a continuous ovation through the whole line of route, the regiment arrived in Chicago, near the close of the day, and marched through the city with the Eagle under the colors. How the scene electrified Chicago! A correspondent of the Eau Claire *Free Press* says:

"Formed in platoons, we took our way through the city, our Colonel and Governor Alex. Randall leading us on horseback.

Our progress was marked by many demonstrations of enthusiasm — the regiment as a whole, and our 'glorious bird' carried
aloft at the head of our company, appearing to divide about
equally the general attention and applause. I fancied the Eagle
seemed for once to be of more importance than the 'Eagles,' and
received cheers and flattering comment enough to spoil any less
sensible bird."

The Chicago *Tribune,* under date of October 13, thus
alludes to the reception:

"A noticeable feature among them was the Chippewa Eagles—
Capt. Perkins' company — a company of the first-class stalwart
fellows. The live Eagle which they brought with them was an
object of much curiosity. He is a majestic bird and well
trained. When marching, the Eagle is carried at the head of
the company, elevated on a perch at the top of a pole. The
Eagle was caught on the head waters of the Chippewa River by
an Indian. Capt. Perkins' company takes it to the war. The
men were offered a large sum for it in Madison, but they will
not part with it. They swear it shall never be taken by the
enemy. No doubt the Chippewa Eagles and their pet bird will
be heard of again."

HERALDRY OF FREEDOM IN ST. LOUIS.

On the morning of the 14th, the regiment arrived at the
Mississippi, opposite St. Louis. The ferry-boat steamed
to the shore and received the "Wisconsin cargo" with
brisk orders. When approaching the city, the band
played the "Star Spangled Banner," hearing which, the
ladies waved their handkerchiefs in proud welcome.
Knowing that Union soldiers had recently been fired
upon by rebel citizens, difficulties were anticipated;
but, what was their surprise, instead of rebels, Union-
ists showed signs of belligerency. What did it mean?
Like the Confederates, our soldiers were then dressed in

gray, and, therefore, were at first taken for a rebel regiment. Though excessively hot, they were obliged to put on their blue overcoats to satisfy the patriotic populace that had been outraged a few days before. When the regiment was preparing to enter one of the principal streets, a promiscuous crowd huddled around, and, seeing the Eagle, cried out, "a crow!" "a wild goose!" "a turkey buzzard!" As if resolved upon a demonstration of defiance to these insults against his highness, "Old Abe," crouching low for a spring, half-poising his wings, sprung impetuous, breaking the cord that held him to his perch, and scud just over the heads of the motley crowd, even flapping a few caps with the tips of his pinions, and, thence shooting higher, sailed up, up, a thousand voices shouting after him, and majestically alighted upon the chimney of an aristocratic mansion. The whole regiment was thrown into excitement, especially company C, that could scarcely be wheeled into rank and file for marching order through the city. In the general confusion, several soldiers sped after their Eagle, scattering in different alleys and constantly watching him on his inaccessible eyrie. The flight heightened the curiosity of the spectators. Being informed it was an Eagle from the North, they were in ecstasies. Meantime, "Old Abe" sat on his new perch of a chimney, leisurely surveying the sea of heads, and, after a half hour's liberty alone in his glory, scooped down to an obscure sidewalk, where he was caught, and thence conveyed to his regiment.

This being the first band of warriors from the North-west, bringing, too, a live Eagle, with the loyal people the reception was magnificent. "The little darkies hurrahed for the Union, and one old 'Dinah,' in particular, will be long remembered, she laughed so heartily, showing her white teeth and 'big eyes,' and crying out at the top of her voice, 'Go in, boys! go in! God bress ye!'" Halting at one of the principal hotels, the regiment was welcomed to the city by Governor Gamble, who, in the course of his patriotic address, frequently pointed to the Eagle, cheered by the soldiers. Arriving at Benton Barracks, they were addressed by Secretary Cameron and Gen. Thomas, who highly complimented them for their fine appearance, with a good word for "Old Abe."

A gentleman in St. Louis offered the company five hundred dollars for the Eagle; and, somewhere in the South, subsequent to this, an Illinoisian offered a valuable farm. Coming up from a bushel of corn! But all proffers of this kind were declined. Capt. Perkins' saying became proverbial — "No money can buy him."

CHAPTER II.

"ON TO THE FRONT."

" For thee they fought, for thee they fell,
    And their oath on thee was laid;
  To thee the clarions raised their swell,
    And the dying warrior prayed.
  Thou wert, thro' an age of death and fears,
    The image of pride and power,
  Till the gathered rage of a thousand years,
    Burst forth in one awful hour."

SCARCELY had the regiment unpacked, ere it was ordered to advance, and, on the evening of the 15th of October, 1861, that inexperienced band rushed forward on their long and perilous adventure. Who could read the future? Could that prophet bird of sun-lighted vision? It was a gala time. At Big River — the bridge burned by the enemy — as the men transported their baggage across on their backs, wading waist deep, the Eagle, noticing the ripples and fishes, whistled a merry note with the rest. The feeling was universal, that no better companion could inspire hilarity and enthusiasm under difficulties. As he led the van of the column, in sight of all the soldiers, over that variegated country, and thence in all their subsequent marches, he was not only a constant reminder of their oath of trust, but of loftiness of ambition. He often played under the waving colors, watching other birds in the far-up blue

where no human eye could penetrate, panting and as-
piring to rise on peerless wing, monarch of all.

"An eagle has the power of altering the focus of his eye just
as he pleases; he has only to look at an object at the distance of
two feet or two miles, in order to see it with perfect distinctness.
The ball of his eye is surrounded by fifteen little plates, called
sclerotic bones; they form a complete ring, and their edges
slightly overlap each other. When he looks at a distant object,
this little circle of bones expands, and the ball of the eye being
relieved from the pressure, becomes flatter; and when he looks at
a very near object, the little bones press together, and the ball of
the eye is thus squeezed into a rounder or more convex form;
the effect is very familiar to everybody; a person with very
round eyes is near-sighted, and only sees clearly an object that
is close to him; and a person with flat eyes, as in old age, can
see nothing clearly except at a distance; the eagle, by the mere
will, can make his eyes round or flat, and see with equal clear-
ness at any distance."

A BATTLE.

A march all night, on the 20th, a sleep in the streets
of Fredericktown, Missouri, till noon, a reinforcement,
and — hark! — the bugle calls; the enemy is discerned
in the woods. There is hot haste; it is such an earnest!
The Eighth is a reserve. Chained on the roof of the court
house, only half a mile distant from the scene of action,
the Eagle sees the rush and line of dark-winged battle.
His trepidation is that of a soldier when going to face
death. There comes the clash of arms, the spurring of
the ambulances, the wounded soldier returned, bleeding, groaning, dying; he is wild with excitement, revel-
ing and tearing, and, one observer says, " gnawing his
perch with his beak," as if crazed at the new exper-

ience, but calms down with the lull of battle — the first victory!

> "There fell a moment's silence round, —
> A breathless pause! — a hush of hearts that beat,
> And limbs that quivered."

"ABE" AND THE DOG "FRANK."

After winter quarters at Sulphur Springs, Mo., "Old Abe" was next seen at Cairo, Ill. Up to this date, January 19, 1862, he had experienced enough of military life to render him stern and heroic. Like the soldiers, he was sure to retaliate injuries ; his motto was American —*justice.* One of his playmates was the dog "Frank," that voluntarily came to the regiment whilst at Madison. The Eagle felt an Epicurean interest in this animal, on account of the spoils of the hunt. Whenever he heard that sharp, familiar bark in the woods, he would bend low his head to catch the welcome sound, for it betokened a fresh meal ; and the moment the canine hunter returned with a squirrel or rabbit in his mouth, such a coaxing from the perch, such a chuckling and rustling of wings, such a grateful "Thank you, Frank !" In the absence of more agreeable company, the soldiers were real Selkirks, whiling away monotonous hours in teaching these pets various cunning tricks. Thus a mutual attachment sprung up between them, constituting at length a "marriage on interest," and quite happily did they live together in their odd association, mutually sharing the patrimony of their friends. But, as is common with such "unions," a divorce took place under the most unfortunate circumstances:

One day there was a constant draft upon his patience;
but this he could have endured, had no one tormented
him with sticks and mockings. Feeling forbearance too
long suffered is no Eagle virtue, he bit, and tore, and
yelled, but could not get near enough to his besiegers
to vindicate his sense of justice. Unfortunately "Frank"
came within the circle of his cord, and, quick as lightning, he pounced upon him, sticking his talons into the
hide, and "making the fur fly." Such a pow-wow was
never before heard in a military camp. Ever after,
"Frank" kept at a respectful distance, and from that
time "Abe" has had an eternal hatred for dogs. He
evidently believed they were not "well mated."

Early the next spring, the "Eagles" moved to New
Madrid, and, on the 11th of March, occupied rifle pits at
Point Pleasant, preventing rebel transportation to Island
No. 10, and frolicking with cannon and shell, "Old
Abe" often sending a scream to the boys from the camp
near by, enjoying the "pegging business" with the
rest. The gunboat "Carondolet" sweeping both shores
of rebel batteries, the island captured, the Eagle chased
the flying enemy, and saw his comrades seize six thousand prisoners, who, beholding this living emblem of
national fealty, "quailed before his piercing look, that
sent the fire of convicting justice to their hearts."

The opening of the Mississippi, by conquest of that
blockade of batteries, nearly to Memphis, was the be-
ginning of a series of victories, so important, Gen. J. B.
Plummer commanding the brigade of the "Eagles," announced the order of Gen. Pope, for all the regiments
and battalions of his command to inscribe on their flag,

"New Madrid and Island No. 10." As "Old Abe" rode under these new colors, he appeared indeed the "Bird of Jove," that "armed the skies."

STRATEGY AT FARMINGTON.

Proud of their achievement, aiming at a test of the strength of the enemy at Corinth, "the Army of the Eagle" sailed up the Ohio and Tennessee rivers, stopping at Pittsburg Landing, where lay the "Blue and the Gray"—peaceful now in half-covered graves. Disembarking at Hamburg, in quest of Gen. Beauregard, they at length formed in line of battle at Farmington, Miss., on the 9th of May, 1862, Maj. Jefferson commanding the outposts. The odds were great—25,000 of the enemy against one brigade. The "Eagles" and 26th Illinois were sent forth to rake the woods. Up rose the foe, quick, sullen, defiant; but these two regiments held the ground for half an hour in that raking fire. Anxious for "Old Abe," Capt. Perkins ordered the Bearer to keep well in the rear, but within hailing distance of his company. As the hosts of the enemy pressed on, nothing could stand before the swath of destruction. Simultaneously, they prostrated themselves on the ground, in the open field behind a knoll, the leaden rain pouring over them. Not being conspicuously exposed, the Bearer determined to remain upright, but the Eagle, seeing the men lying there, imitated their example. He was picked up, with stern orders to keep his perch, but refused to obey. This experiment was tried five or six times. Giving him his own way, "Jim" at last threw the perch on the ground, and crouched low

3

with the rest, when the Eagle crept close to his side, remaining so till, at the bugle sound, he leaped voluntarily to his perch with the rising of the men, a signal of heroism through all the battle. The author of a little work, entitled "Army Life and Stray Shots from a Staff Officer of the Eighth Regiment Wisconsin Volunteers," thus describes this scene:

"At the battle of Farmington, May 9, 1862, the men were ordered to lie down. The instant they did so, it was impossible to keep him upon his perch. He insisted on being protected as well as they, and, when liberated, flattened himself on the ground, and there remained till the men arose; when, with outspread wings, he resumed his place of peril and held it till the close of the contest."

David McLane, a member of company C, says, in a letter dated "Camp near Vicksburg, Miss., Feb. 18, 1865:

"The first fight the Eagle was in was the battle of Farmington, Miss., where he showed a great deal of sagacity. When we were ordered to lie down on the ground, under a dreadful artillery fire from the enemy's batteries, he flew off his perch, getting as low as he could, and lay there until he saw the regiment rise to advance, when he flew upon his perch again, and remained there through the engagement."

In this battle fell Capt. Perkins, mortally wounded — a brave soldier and true patriot — Lieut. Victor Wolf succeeding in command. In his report, Gen. Palmer highly complimented the "Regiment that bore the Eagle."

"Old Abe" was in the battle before Corinth, on the 28th of May. As the whole army sent up its shout at sight of the Union flag on the enemy's works, he, the heraldry of the victory, was seen "whirling and dancing on his perch." Battles made him voracious. A soldier avers that, soon after the cheering, while he was eating a rabbit, the bugle of his regiment calling to pursue the enemy, a convalescent soldier ordered him to mount his standard, when, as if appreciating the urgency of the moment, "Old Abe" devoured the remaining half with one swallow, and leaped to his perch. wiping his beak as he rode to the colors, saying. in his manner, "Well equipped, boys!" When at the front, the question rose, "Who shall carry the Eagle?" his Bearer being sick. Among the many voluntary applicants, Capt. Wolf selected Thomas J. Hill, of Eau Claire, remarking, "Tom is worthy of it." Shouldering his living musket, "Tom," in his hurry to keep up, unavoidably entered a clump of bushes, where "Old Abe" initiated his new Bearer into the apprenticeship of the "perch business." Getting entangled, he tore away exasperated, but was hustled up rather roughly, when, wishing to give his master a trial of his military patience, "Abe" stuck his talons into his face; but no court martial was held!

UNDERGOING DISCIPLINE.

Scattering the enemy, "Old Abe's" brigade went into summer quarters near Clear Creek, in a charming locality. Here he attended his "military school." The live long days he busied himself — running at large — catching crazy bugs with his claws in puddles of water, fishing by "make-believes" in the creek, catching bullets rolled upon the ground, running off with the ball in the hilarious game, tipping over water pails, visiting

the sutler's tent, tearing up the soldiers' clothes there
hung upon the line, with no chance for indemnity, for
"too much indulgence spoils the child," and "the conquering party dictates terms." One day a soldier cut
off the heads of some chickens, and left them a few
moments to flutter, while preparing to cook them, when
"Old Abe" noticed the movement at a little distance
down the street, and slily hurried to the spot, passing
some soldiers, who warned the cook of the foraging
attitude; and as the man turned to look for his chickens in one direction, "Abe," perceiving one in the grass
just behind him, snatched it up and whirled off like a
rocket, amid the jeers of the spectators, the cook just
behind, puffing and swearing, unable to secure scarcely
enough for the captain's meal. He "went in swim-
ming" with the "other soldiers." During one of these
water frolics, Mr. Hill was accosted by a semi-Unionist
farmer, who offered to give the Eagle a chicken, if
shown to his children. Arriving at the house, among
them appeared a fair young lady who vainly coaxed the
bird for the privilege of only touching his kingly
plumage, remarking, she "never expected to see the
celebrated Eagle which the Confederate soldiers say is
carried by a Yankee regiment." Soon "Old Abe" was
set at liberty among the fowls, when, after the style of
a lion — a peculiarity of habit always noticed on such
occasions — he threw his head from side to side, walked
around his selected victim with a stealthy air, and made
his terrible lunge; missing it, he measured the distance
again with his geometric eye, and succeeded. Drawing
the chicken directly under him, and standing defiantly

upon it, he opened his wings to a hovering motion, bent down his tail spread out like a fan, rustled up his feathers, and uttered a vengeful satisfaction; these incantations over, he plunged his beak into the heart, and devoured it palpitating. Looking on and shuddering. the children exclaimed "Oh! Mister!—Oh!" But "Tom" gave the beautiful brunette a significant wink, saying: "He is from old Wisconsin; you see how he likes the South!"

Unless extremely hungry, "Old Abe" never eats anything tainted or decayed. He enjoys his meals best if allowed to kill his own game. If he rejects anything from his perch, he frequently looks down at it with a dignified scorn. He drinks like a hen; but, during war time, when no better chance availed itself, he would throw back his head, open his mouth, and permit his Bearer to pour the water down his throat from a canteen.

To the soldiers he served as a barometer. If the weight of the atmosphere indicated a storm, he was uneasy to find a shelter ere it came on, and, if secured, was very lively. No one but his Bearer could approach him then without an Eagle's severe reproof; for they were his sacred hours of communion with the Boreau gods, when his every motion said, "No admission, gentlemen, except on military business." If the lightning flashed, his eye was lighted with a new fury; and, as the thunder followed, he would listen with rapt suspense, and then scream aloud in terrible revelry for a few minutes; but as the rain beat steady and heavy, he would grow calm, and, hiding his head under his wing, "sweetly snoring," await the sunshine.

"Abe" would shake hands with his Bearer, grasp the fingers in his bill, pressing harder, chuckling, "Does it hurt?" Very sensitive as to his rights, he resented every abuse, and never forgot it. One day a sergeant tormented him with rough handling, and affronted him by mimicking his manner of self-defense; and, like an Indian, he laid up a store of vengeance for him. When the sergeant returned, several months afterwards, from a journey, "Abe" fixed his eye upon him, and, the moment he came into his presence, flew at his head with fury, and actually drove him off. It takes an Eagle to teach some men the laws of etiquette.

CHASING THE NEGRO.

One day, just after a bath in the creek, a negro addressed the Eagle in a rough style, tormenting him; in an instant he was after the "young sauce box," his eyes darting fire, his claws protruding, his beak wide open, his feathers ruffled to wrath. By striking his wings upon the ground, and springing on his elastic feet, he leaped after his assailant with engine speed, accompanied with a revengeful screech. Hotter and hotter grew the race, the negro gaining advantage only by turning short corners. "Hurrah! Nig!" shouted the laughing soldiers, enjoying the fun. Looking back with a side glance, he caught a glimpse of that awful mouth extended close to his head, when, dodging downwards, the infuriated bird just grazed his wool. The negro was more respectful after that race; a lesson we all should learn, never to insult the American Eagle!

At Camp Clear Creek a change of bearers was ordered.

Mr. Hill being appointed to a regimental position, it was tendered David McLane, of Menomonie, Wis., on the 18th of August, 1862.

IUKA.

Towards the close of summer, an army three miles long, "Old Abe" this time in the rear, marched into northern Alabama and rendezvoused in beautiful Tuscumbia, famous for its mineral springs, " where charming ladies in their teens, well trained by their loyal mothers, pointed their tiny fingers at our Eagle, making mouths prettily, and wanted to know if we called it Yank! Yank!"

It is the 18th of September, 1862. It is daylight; the army is stirring. The forces are concentrating on Iuka. Stanley is there; Oglesby, Ord, the Wisconsin Hamilton, Hackleman, Kirby Smith, "the "Eagles," "Old Abe," Rosecrans commanding, — these are there. There is a moment of perturbation. Who shall report a soldier's look-out of soul to the gathering storm, as he thinks of home? Who can register for the pondering ages coming, how civilizations hung upon the issues of a great battle ? Who can tell the chancery angel of the reckoning day in the eternal world, what feelings throbbed in the bosoms of Northern and Southern mothers, as their sons, the noblest of the country, there met in deadly grapple ? Oh, those three hours of unceasing conflict, sword to sword, bayonet to bayonet, trampling brothers under feet ! A nation hears that awful clash of arms ; it is victory at last, and the war Eagle sends its news that night in a wild scream over the martyrs.

Though the dead lay in heaps, no harm befell him ; he was carried safely through by McLane.

On the same day of the Iuka victory, at Jackson, Tenn., expired James McGennis, the 1st Eagle Bearer. He carried the Eagle through the battles of Fredericktown, New Madrid and Farmington.

ATTEMPT OF GEN. PRICE TO CAPTURE "OLD ABE."

ON discovering that the enemy was concentrating for a grand attack on Corinth, then held by our forces, Rosecrans rallied his hosts on the 3d of October, 1862, to meet the issue against 42,000 Southern troops combined under Price, Van Dorn and Lovell. In the attempt to gain the brow of a hill overlooking the town, the rebels charged upon our lines with a yell and dash, but were promptly met by a wall of adamant that turned the tide. Again they formed and hurled themselves forward like an angry wave of the sea to capture our batteries, but were repulsed. At this time the "Eagles" stood near the base of the hill, clear in front of the line, "Old Abe" in the regimental advance. Before the battle commenced, Gen. Price having heard of the Eagle and his fame, and, knowing his capture would electrify the South, ordered his men to take him at any hazard.

A staff officer of the regiment, who was not only an eye witness but an actor in this battle, says: "At the battle of Corinth, the rebel Gen. Price, having discovered him, ordered his men to be sure and take him; if this they could not do, to kill him, adding he had rather get that bird than the whole brigade." David McLane, in his letter of the 18th February, 1865, also says:

"The rebel Gen. Price saw him there and ordered his men either to capture, or kill him, at all hazards, stating that he had heard of that bird before, and would rather capture him than the whole brigade. I had this statement from rebel prisoners and believe it to be true."

Col. J. W. Jefferson, furnishing valuable facts for this work, verifies what others have testified:

"One of Gen. Price's men, who was captured by us, told me, Price said to his men that he would rather have them capture the Eagle of the 8th Wisconsin than a '*dozen battle-flags*,' and that if they succeeded, he would give the lucky (or unlucky) Confederate 'Free Pillage in Corinth!' The valiant rebels did not succeed, however, but, instead, many of them were captured."

A rebel soldier, brother of a guerilla chief, visiting Madison, in 1875, informed Geo. W. Baker, one of the Eagle's attendants, that, while in the Southern service, during one of the battles, he heard a rebel general say, "I rather capture 'Old Abe' than a whole brigade."

During a lull in the battle, as the enemy was preparing again to fire from the brow of the hill, distant not over thirty rods from the Eighth regiment, the Eagle being exposed in plain sight of the rebels. a Confederate officer was heard by several in company C to say "There he is — the Eagle — capture him, boys!" No sooner was this command given, than the rebel artillery opened upon our forces, under whose cover a column just discerned in the gathering smoke, moved briskly over the crest to break and scatter our steady front, and capture the prize. All this while, the Eagle scanned with fire-lit eye every movement on that hill, and as the rebel infantry hove clear out in sight, he, it is said, whistled a

startling note of alarm, and instantly both armies struck
each other in deafening shock, commingling with the
boom and crash of cannon that trembled forest and
valley.   Shouts from both sides rent the air, while death
mowed his swath clear through both armies, and yet the
bloody gaps closed up again and again.   Such is war!
In the general conflict, the Eagle leaped up with a desperate spring, breaking his cord or else it was cut by a
Minie ball, and was seen by the combatants, circling,
careering in the sulphurous smoke.   The enemy pressed
nearer, exultant, as if sure of their prize; the bullets
flew as hailstones; there was a wavering of a wing —
was he hit? — but the war-bird rallied again, and, as he
rose higher, many a rebel shot went up to bring down
the American Eagle! — but on he sped, towering above
that awful din, screaming back to his assailants, eyeing
the battle from his sky-eyrie, when, catching a glimmer
of his comrades in the fight and the colors where his
Bearer stood gazing upward with suspense — as if inspired by the very Roman gods — he descended, like a
" bolt of Jove," to the left of his regiment, where Mc-
Lane, flying after him, easily caught him up in his arms,
trembling and panting with ardor, and whistling
with his peculiar air of satisfaction.   By permission,
his Bearer immediately carried him cautiously from the
field to the camp, where he remained till the close of
the next day of battle, which ended in a Federal victory
purchased at a dear cost.   On examination, it was found
that the Eagle was hit by a rebel bullet in the feathers
of a wing near the flesh.

" If a Roman army were defeated, the eagle was not suffered

to fall into the hands of the enemy; when the standard-bearer saw the rout begin, he broke his lance in twain, and buried in the earth that portion which was crowned by the imperial symbol. This took place after the fatal battle of Lake Thrasymene; and we owe to such a precaution the only legionary eagle that has been preserved to our times. It was found in Germany on the land of the Count d'Erlach; is of bronze gilt, three inches high, and weighs eight pounds. It is supposed to have belonged to the 22d legion, which being sorely pressed in a battle with the Alemanni, the eagle-bearer, before he took to flight, concealed in the earth the precious symbol intrusted to his care."

Theirs was the reverential respect of the Roman soldiery. Many a correspondent of the army, writing home about this attempt of Gen. Price to capture " Old Abe," threw out the challenge — " Let him come and take him!" They would have shot and buried the Eagle in the midst of a battle, rather than permit him to fall into the hands of the enemy.

CROPPING THE EAGLE.

Soon after the battle of Corinth, some one in the regiment had the dastardly audacity to crop the tail and a wing of the Eagle, to prevent his flying away during an engagement. It was argued by the shabby party concerned, that he "might get lost." After all, he could soar into a tree, but he no longer looked like himself; and much did his appearance mortify the soldiers generally and regimental officers. Disgusted with the treatment of his bird, McLane resigned his Eagle commission, on the 1st of Nov., 1862, when Edward Homaston, of Eau Claire, was tendered the honor. Having been reared among the Green Mountains of Vermont, where in boyhood he watched the eagles' flights every day, he took to "Old Abe" with a natural instinct. Their friendship for one another was very strong; indeed, "Ed" and "Abe" were brothers, thoroughly understanding each other.

THE EAGLE'S VERNACULAR.

Mr. Homaston translated the Eagle's idiom into English. He found "Old Abe" varies his voice according to emotions. When surprised, he whistles a wild melody, toned to a melancholy softness; when hovering over his food, he gives a spiteful chuckle; when pleased to see an old friend, he says a "how do you do?" with a plaintive cooing. His scream in battle was wild, commanding, uttering five or six notes in succession with a most startling trill that was perfectly inspiring to the soldiers. Strangers could never approach and touch him with safety, but those of his regiment that treated him with courtesy, he was ever glad to see. David McLane says:

"He has his particular friends and his enemies. There were men in our company whom he would not let come near him; on them he would fly, and tear them with his talons and beak in a way not very pleasant; but he would never fight his Bearer. He knew his own regiment from any other, and would always cheer with it, but never for any other regiment during the war."

MORALE OF APPETITE.

Late in the fall of 1862, Gen. Grant, then commanding the Mississippi Division, formed an expedition to gain the rear of Vicksburg and use up Price in his retreat. Our war Eagle was in that imposing army, the recognized signal of success. Passing through Grand

Junction, Tenn., thence over a country infested with guerilla hordes, they arrived at Cold Water early in the winter, and, chilled, fatigued and hungry, prepared for encampment. After they had fairly stacked arms, and were leisurely resting in various attitudes, "Old Abe," whose wings were yet "a little awry," as if understanding the laws of regimental hygiene by dispelling a camp gloom, broke his cord and awkwardly flew for the woods, drawing after him a goodly number of his regiment, running in different directions. A soldier climbed the tree in which he had alighted, and, catching him, threw him roughly to the ground, when up he flew, enraged, into another. This time they tried to bring him down by throwing clubs and stones at him. As was his custom at play, these he caught with his claws; one of them caused his mouth to bleed profusely, and he was stubborn. Finding that method useless, they procured a live chicken, tied it with a long string to the tree, and thus tempted him to docility. After that stampede, they never forgot the moral of the incident — that the persuasion of the appetite is better than brute force.

ANOTHER COQUETTISH FLIGHT.

On the 5th of December, the "Eagles" encamped at Waterford, on the Tallahatchie River. The Eagle's camp was a beautiful bower under the hollies, and there "Abe" and "Ed" slept together. The author of 'Opening of the Mississippi" says:

"The 12th Wisconsin, Col. Bryant, is encamped about half a mile from us (at Waterford). As his regiment was passing our last camp a few days ago, the Eighth brought out the Eagle, and formed in line by the roadside. As they caught a glimpse of our old bird, they commenced cheering; and many here found friends and relations whom they had not seen for over a year."

As the Colonel made a brief speech, recounting the hardships they had mutually endured, and the justice of their cause, the Eighth cheering, "Old Abe," jumping up and down on his perch, sprung with such force, the cord broke, and away he sped, soaring into the ether in gay life. When he had satisfied his ambition, he gently descended to a distant tree top, where the daring Philip Burk captured and returned him thence to the regiment.

" YANKEE BUZZARD ! "

When fairly ready to enjoy the new homes at Waterford, marching orders came to "move on to Oxford." Disappointed, but faithful to duty, they promptly obeyed, and in one week reached the place, through which they marched in platoons. When fairly in the principal street, "a lady of the Emerald Isle" coolly asked, "Why don't you shoot that *buzzard?*" Going a few rods further, a young Miss, standing on the sidewalk with the crowd, gaily attired, inquired, "What is that bird you carry?" On being informed, "It is an American Eagle," she replied, "You can't fool *me;* that is a turkey buzzard!" Turning a corner, and keeping a steady lookout, another lady, "of decidedly Southern origin, rushed from a stately mansion by the wayside, with arms extended and hair streaming wildly in the wind, and, with scornful sarcasm, exclaimed, ' Oh, see that Yankee Buzzard !' " By this time the soldiers concluded a return fire would not be inapplicable, and a hundred voices shouted back, "' *Where is your Southern Pelican?*' in so unmistakable emphasis, that she retreated for the house on double quick." As the regiment remained there about a week, keeping provost guard, all such inquisitors soon learned the species of the bird when first " they met his terrible eyes of justice to rebellion." Some boys there, it is said, provoked the Eagle and annoyed the soldiers. One day, a little boy, with bare feet, approached the bird, then on the ground. The boy's feet, by much exposure, were about the color of a toad's back, and about the size, in general appearance, of average specimens of those amphibia. The Eagle began to turn his head right and left, peering at them.

"Take care of your feet, boy," said one of the men. "The Eagle will pounce on them, if you don't stand back."

"Oh, I guess not," said another. "He isn't hungry now. We fed him a small boy a little while ago."

The boy took a retrograde movement without further delay ; and, after that, he and his grade of mates kept at a respectful distance from the Eagle.

"SEE DAT YANKEE BIRD!"

Flying, on the 20th, to Tallahatchie, on the cars, there skirmishing with the enemy, reinforced with 5,000 troops, marching thence eighteen miles, resting that night on the cold sods, with "bayonets for their wives," they rose with the dawn of the 21st, and stood on a hill overlooking Holly Springs, all spread out to view in grand perspective, when, simultaneously, the whole army sent up a jubilant shout that startled the people in every street. "Old Abe," beholding the scene, exulting in the enthusiasm, joined his shrill voice as the addenda always of military rejoicing. Price had occupied that city the day before, having sacked the town and made good his escape; and now came the Northerners, with banners unfurled to the breeze, headed by martial music, and the Eagle at his post in heraldic dignity, marching into that proud, beautiful city. "Abe" was the observed of all observers, "and not a few negroes," says Mr. Driggs, "overwhelmed with joy at the sight of 'Linkum's army come to sabe us,' swung their hats, and, nudging one another, exclaimed, 'See dat Yankee Bird!' whilst the 'secesh ladies' peeped through the window shutters, and, with scornful lips, hissed at the saviors of American liberty!"

Being now on the track of Price — doubtless his comrades will ever remember the "Eagle Regiment" — brigaded with the 17th and 32d Wisconsin and 93d Indiana, they chased him in zigzag directions, day and night, weary, and everywhere imperiled, but never despairing. "Old Abe," in this swift pursuit, was on his war perch, with head to windward, and wings flapping backward to speed the journey. He was more quiet at night when on the march, constantly on the watch, alive to every sound, invariably informing his Bearer of any danger from a limb of a tree, or of the enemy, by an alarm note of surprise. Even when the army rested at night, if any one approached, however cautiously, he would suddenly withdraw his head from under his wing and make a complaining screech, indicating he did not care to be disturbed. Like a revolutionary "minute man," he seemed to calculate for the morrow's march, by resting when all was safe, conscious of protection from faithful pickets. His quick ear detected the tread of the enemy; a sharp note and tremor of nerve unmistakably warned the army to be vigilant.

Poor and forlorn were those faithful soldiers when they arrived at Grand Junction, on the 23d, having had no sleep for three nights, and being without tents, blankets or covering of any kind. The Eagle felt all the emotions of his comrades, and actually whined to his Bearer, with a most searching plea for food. Every body refusing his importunities for "pity on the Eagle," Homaston sought the first hen roost convenient for forage, satisfied that the "military necessity" of "Abe's" voracious stomach demanded even the last chicken of the Confederacy to "save the Union!"

"ABE" AND THE GUINEA HEN.

Again changing front to rear, "Abe" was next domesticated, on the 24th of December, at La Grange, Tenn. Here no meat could be procured for our Eagle. Capt. Wolf made several unsuccessful attempts to buy a chicken of a semi-Unionist. Getting spunky over it, he took the Bearer and his hungry bird with him one day to that gentleman's house, and, by a porter, made the same demand as before; and the same provoking denial was returned. Learning that the Captain had the Eagle there under threat to let him (the bird) select his own chicken, "the half-and-half loyalist" came out, and to

4

compromise the matter, offered a Guinea hen, provided
the Eagle could kill her in a fair fight.   About this time
quite a crowd had gathered, among which were several
regimental officers, to witness "the battle of birds."
Eying his prey with a measuring glance, "Abe" sprung
forward, when the hen uttered her peculiar squall—
a sound altogether new to his quick ear—which so
startled him that he paused for further examination.
Improving this "cessation of hostilities," she scud off
to the opposite corner, "facing the music."   Enraged at
such procedure, the Eagle made another dash, which
was followed by the same unearthly squall, and this by
another pause.   There was no possibility of outflanking
the hen, neither did she dare to meet him in "mortal
combat," so round and round they flew, amid roars of
laughter, neither of the "flying squadrons" the victor,
till at length Madame Guinea escaped into a chink under a building, where Monsieur Eagle could not penetrate.   The general fun evoked a fellow feeling ; and
"Old Abe" was next permitted to seize a fat shanghai
with one unerring spring, when the grave looking
"Abraham" enjoyed a feast.

"COTTON IS KING."

At La Grange, "Abe's" rendezvous was a fort composed of cotton bales, which furnished him new amusement.   "Cotton is King !" said the Southrons, for nearly a century, and Church and State bowed to this Moloch
of Slavery, whose foot was upon our sable brother, pressing out the bloody sweat to refresh the famished Eden
of the West ; but our "Bird of Liberty," inspired with

the free idea of the age, evidently disdained the "King," and proved that despot was only "stuffed cotton," after all, as he tore it out with a frolicking chuckle, and trod it under his feet for a soft bed to lie on in the sun. On Christmas day of 1862, the soldiers hoisted an immense flag on these works, and then gave three rousing cheers for the Union. "Old Abe" was standing at the time right under it, close to the staff. When the last cheer died away, he gave his startling war-scream with trilling vibrations, when another shout went up in a general "Hurrah for the Soldier Bird of Wisconsin !"

"BRAVO, OLD ABE."

Vibrating back to the old battle grounds of Corinth, and thence to Germantown, Tenn., the "Eagles" there made a church their headquarters, during the remainder of the winter. Whether it was because of fashion, or a sense of religious duty, the boys do not report. but "it was most comical to see him going to church to *prey* so earnestly !"

On the 11th of March, 1863, they were ordered to Memphis — most welcome news, for they anticipated a rest amid the gayeties and luxuries of city life. "Old Abe" remained on his perch all that day, watching the preparation ; becoming impatient the next morning, and evidently thinking so long delay in filling an order unlike "the swift Eagles," the moment he heard the blast of the bugle, so electrifying was it to his patriotic nerve, he snatched up the cord, then stiffened by a recent cold rain, and bit it in two clear and smooth, as if cut by a knife, and, to signify "Come on, boys, it is high time to

march," soared over the regiment with a whir of exul-
tation, high, higher, on easy wing, sailing round and
round in the dark sky, and when up to a shooting point,
scooped far off in a grand circle, and back over the army
again, the whole brigade gazing, and thousands of voices
shouting, "Bravo, Old Abe!" They could not march
without their pet bird, and as the whole army paused
in the general excitement, Homaston, flying with the
rest, requested the frantic fellows to keep cool while he
and a German lad would surely capture him at his old
watering place, where he had then alighted. Approaching cautiously, he put the perch at the right angle, and
coaxing him to mount, at length secured him fast.
When returned to the regiment, amid acclamations, the
bugle sounded again, and "Abe," with the rogue in his
eyes, and patriotism in his air of dignity, said, "Steady,
sir, go on!"

CONFEDERATE RESPECT.

When at Memphis, certain Confederate citizens gave
Mr. Homaston money to purchase meat for his Eagle.
They respected the living emblem of that Union for
which they had a heart, though conventionally arrayed
against it. The following clipping from the diary of
Joseph Lawton, Sergeant of Company K., who kept a
record of all the army movements, shows how earnest
was the respect at Memphis:

"On Steamer 'Empress,' Memphis, Tenn., *March* 14, 1863.

"Yesterday afternoon, as we marched through the city of Memphis to embark on this steamer, the regiment and the *live Eagle*
attracted great attention, as usual, and many red, white and
blue flags, and white handkerchiefs saluted us on our march."

Their "long rest" at Memphis was only for a few days. The order was imperative — to Helena, the "Soldiers' Sepulchre." "Old Abe" did not like the journey; steamboats and "mule wagons" were his disgust. When arrived at Yazoo Pass, while the boys were freighting the "Ben Franklin" with war equipments, the rain poured in torrents, and the wind "blew like a southern hurricane," before which the trees fell crashing all around the men. In the desperate struggles to save his life, "Old Abe" got the cord so awkwardly around him, that he was actually hung in a tree; and one of his legs was much bruised, laming him for several weeks.

Landing at Ducksport, near Young's Point, on the 1st of April, 1863, they went into camp on the Louisiana side, only nine miles above Vicksburg and two miles above the famous fleet anchored there to subdue the city, employing their time digging canals, building roads, and preparing steamers to run the blockade. Here they were addressed one day by Gen. Thomas, Adj. Gen. U. S. A., and, during his patriotic remarks, he feelingly alluded to the immortal Emancipation Proclamation of President Lincoln, ordering the freedom and enlistment of negroes, and urged that such deserving privates as their officers might recommend, should present themselves as candidates for commanders in colored regiments and companies. As his eye glanced over the stalwart ranks, he caught a view of "Old Abe," whom he had not seen since the greeting in St. Louis, about two years before; and, with a new luster firing his vision so tense and determined, he added, "I supposed that all present were strangers to me, but I see one familiar personage at least — that majestic Eagle of the 8th Wisconsin, the emblem now of universal freedom in the Republic."

In Gen. Tuttle's Division, marching, countermarching, through Richmond, La., camping on Smith's Plantation, on Perkins' Plantation, on the shore of Lake St. Joseph — everywhere encouraged by the negroes who thanked " de Lor' that massa Linkum's army hab delibered us from slabery " — they reached Hard Times Landing, on the 7th of May, when, just as each company had stacked arms in the middle of the road, Generals Mower, Smith, Sherman and Grant came dashing by, inspecting the army, and, as they passed the old Eighth, they doffed their hats to the Eagle, at which the regiment cheered, and the bird responded with patriotic civility by his wings and inimitable voice.

Crossing the Mississippi on a gunboat, marching thence to Grand Gulf, to Fort Gibson, to Rocky Springs, the "Eagles" skirmished, on the 12th, with the enemy at Fourteen Mile Creek. Here Gen. Sherman, frequently riding with his staff during the day in their rear, and noticing the dash and skill of those brave men driving the rebels with easy adroitness, afterwards paid them a high compliment, remarking, " You are worthy to carry the American Eagle, and proud must that bird be that is so honored." The next day, entering Raymond, our Eagle witnessed another skirmish, driving the enemy to Mississippi Springs; " and it was fun," says a soldier, " to see how drolly he watched the ' butternuts' as they skedaddled into the tangled brush."

CHARGE ON JACKSON.

On the 14th of May, 1863, Gen. Grant, with his gallant army, stood before Jackson, Mississippi, McPherson at the head of the right wing, and Sherman the left in which the Eagle was placed. A violent storm poured out its vials of wrath upon friend and foe. Gazing at the heavens, the eyes of the Eagle seemed as lightning; and as the clouds pealed forth their fiery thunders, commingling with the roar of cannon, shell and musketry, he was indeed the embodiment of a sublime fury. The boys say, "the lightnings played upon his pinions," and that when he stretched them forth and dashed the electric drops of rain upon the soldiers, they were inspired with an inexpressible enthusiasm. Swift as a mountain avalanche, swifter, swiftest, was that " Forward!"— the "Eagles" led by the intrepid Col. Robbins — until it became the acceleration of Jupiter's bolts, hurling with resistless weight against the enemy, bravely defending his entrenchments. A creek was before the Federal forces; unheeding, they plunged into it — the Eagle carried aloft on his standard — and ploughed across, backing the swelling current till it rose to the waist, and, springing up the opposite bank by the aid of the advance party, the last up pulling out his next neighbor, they formed again, and, in a wild " Eagle yell," swept over a level tract like a dark, whirling tornado, right on to the guns of the enemy in the woods. Nothing on earth could withstand that charge. The rebels fired, fought like brave men well, but, quailing at last, fled amazed. The " Eagles " with their screaming bird were among the first to enter the city. Amid the wild

huzzas of the victors, they flew through the streets, just
as Gen. Joe Johnston with 8,000 men retreated out in a
southernly direction; and, reaching the Capitol, in a moment tore down the rebel flag and hoisted the "stars
and stripes" on the same staff, when cheer upon cheer,
louder, yet louder, "lifted the delivered city," says
one of the more enthusiastic, " a hundred feet into the
victorious air, when 'Old Abe' showed those old sin-
ners how to proclaim liberty throughout all the land."
The battle lulled to a repose, dread and pensive over the
"slain of the daughter of my people;" and there, too,
hovered the Northern Eagle, conscious of a dearly purchased victory, perched on his starry shield just on the
steps in front of the Capitol where was quartered the
Union army. What a contrast of occupancy! what a
retribution in example ever to be remembered as a lesson to nations, that oppression reacts to destruction!
A gentleman from the North, visiting the city of Jackson, in 1860, just before the war broke out, and, standing
before that same State House, saw a large body of people
assembled in the Capitol Park, witnessing and partici-
pating in the sale of slaves at auction, belonging to a
planter that had recently died: " As I stood there, an
intelligent, good looking negro, about twenty-two years
old, occupied a stone pedestal at the side of the front
steps of the Capitol, the auctioneer selling him off to
the highest bidder." One year, over two years of
bloodshed, and the sons of brave mothers from the
North possess that Capitol by force, every room and
chamber honored by Yankee Soldiers, the true flag
floating from the dome, the Eagle that our Revolution-

ary Fathers chose for their and our national emblem, flapping his wings and screaming his terrible war-cry of victory from the very spot where three years before stood that auctioneer selling a human being for gold!

APPEARANCE OF "OLD ABE" IN BATTLE.

Jackson evacuated and needlessly left almost a desolation, the elated army following up its conquest, Napoleon-like, carried its victor Eagle clear through the enemy's ranks at Black River Bridge and Champion Hills, on the 16th, driving those outposts closer to the doomed city. The constant excitement of march and battle, of the hurrying and affrighted populace, roused all the native fire and inspiration of our military bird. His appearance was perfectly magnificent. To be seen in all his glory was when the battle commenced. At the sound of the regimental bugle, which he had learned to recognize, however engaged he might be, he would start suddenly, dart up his head, and then bend it gracefully, anticipating the coming shock; and, when conscious of its reality, his eyes would flash with uncommon luster. Then, with a silent, excited, animation, he would survey the moving squadrons, and, as they rushed into line, his breast would tremble like the human heart, intensified to warring action between hope and fear — an undaunted suspense — a blending of caution and courage — a precipitancy of will, inspiring and sublime. *Click* would go a thousand locks, and he would turn again, curving that majestic neck, scrutinizing the ranks, and dipping his brow forward to await the crash ; and when it came, rolling fiery thunder over the plain, he would

spring up and spread his pinions, uttering his startling
scream, heard, felt and gloried in by the desperate soldiers. As the smoke enveloped him, he would appear
to be bewildered for a moment, but when it opened
again, folding up from the soldiers like a curtain, he
would look down intently, as if inquiring, "How goes
the battle, boys?   What of that last charge?"

"As the engagement waxed hot," says the Washington *Chroni-
cle*, "as the roar of the heavy guns shook the earth, and the rat-
tle of small arms pierced the dim and sulphurous cloud that
hung about the line of battle — the Eagle would flap his wings
and mingle his voice with the tumult in the fiercest and wildest
of his screams."

"When the battle is commenced," says a newspaper correspondent, "the Eagle, with spread pinions, jumps up and down
on his perch, uttering such wild, fearful screams as an eagle
alone can utter. The fiercer and louder the storm of battle, the
fiercer, wilder and louder the screams. What a grand history
he will have — what a grand Eagle he will be a hundred years
hence! Pilgrims will come from all parts of the world to see
the Eagle that was borne through this, our second war for Independence."

"When the battle raged most fiercely," says *Harpers' Weekly*,
"and the enthusiasm of the soldiers was at its highest, then it
was that 'Old Abe' seemed to be in his own element. He flapped
his wings in the midst of the furious storm, and, with head
erect, faced the flying bullets and the crashing shells with no
no signs of fear. 'Old Abe' triumphs with the triumph of the
flag, and seems in some measure conscious of his relationship
with the emblem of a victorious Republic."

Col. J. W. Jefferson, who led the gallant Eighth in
many of its battles, thus describes the war Eagle on
parade and in battle:

"'Old Abe' was with the command in nearly every action.

He enjoyed the excitement; and I am convinced, from his peculiar manner, he was well informed in regard to army movements, dress parade and preparations for the march and battle. Upon parade, after he had been a year in the service, he always gave heed to '*attention!*' With his head obliquely to the front, his right eye directly turned upon the parade commander, he would listen and obey orders, noting time accurately. After parade had been dismissed, and the ranks were being closed by the sergeants, he would lay aside his soldierly manner, flap his wings, and make himself generally at home. When there was an order to form for battle, he and the colors were first upon the line. His actions upon those occasions were uneasy, turning his head anxiously from right to left, looking to see when the line was completed. Soon as the regiment got ready, faced and put in march, he would assume a steady and quiet demeanor. In battle he was almost constantly flapping his wings, having his mouth wide open, and many a time would scream with wild enthusiasm. This was particularly so at the hard-fought battle of Corinth, when our regiment repulsed and charged, or, you might say, made a counter-charge on Price's famous Missouri brigade."

"The Eagle seems," writes David McLane, "to have a dread, like all old soldiers, of heavy musketry; but is in all his glory when the roar of artillery commences. I have had him up to batteries when they were firing into the rebel ranks as fast as they could load, and then he would scream, spread his wings at every discharge, and revel in the smoke and roar of the big guns."

Nor was "Old Abe" indifferent to the casualties of war. When a poor soldier was wounded and bleeding, just fallen, he would often give attention and watch his comrade till carried from the field.

REPENTING AT SIGHT OF THE EAGLE.

The effect of "Old Abe's" personal presence, about this time, was peculiarly salutary. A correspondent of the Chicago *Journal,* writing from Lane, Illinois, thus pictures a battle (fought May 16, 1863), aimed at a closer encirclement of Vicksburg, that decided the fate of the city:

"At Champion Hills — a terrible struggle — the gallant regiment was sorely pressed, and the iron hail poured down on the heroes like a tempest. The Eagle took wing. Up — up — he soared above the smoke of the battle, his screaming piercing the roar of the strife and nerving each loyal arm with new strength and weakening that of the foe. The latter saw and heard, and recognized an augury of defeat."

As the Roman eagle was venerated as an expiatory sacrifice to the guilty soldier, or prisoner, who clasped the lance of the standard bearer, and then was pardoned, for it signified repentance and fealty; so the brave Southron, misguided, when standing in the presence of our Eagle, felt the smiting of national conscience, and there and then the two enemies hailed each other as brothers again.

Lieut. Lansing, in a letter dated at Aurora, Ill., addressed to the New York *Ledger,* gives the following significant incident:

"The only time I ever saw the Eagle was at the rear of Vicksburg, just before it was carried on the field at Champion Hills, during which engagement he was seen by thousands of soldiers, both Federal and rebel. There are many stories circulating among the soldiers relative to the sensations and sad, regretful longings for loyalty and peace excited in the rebel soldier's heart, on beholding the American Eagle hovering its avenging army. To listen to them as told by the private soldier, while sitting by his camp-fire, they are intensely interesting to the loyal mind, and I wish I had the power to reproduce them with equal effect; but my pen must acknowledge its weakness.

There is one incident, however, that came under my own observation. A large wooden building in the rear of the field at 'Big Black Bridge' was filled with rebel wounded, and after our own soldiers' wounds were dressed, I was sent thither for duty. While extracting a ball from a rebel's leg, I was much surprised to find it *round*, and a buck-shot imbedded in the flesh with it, an indication of having come from rebel guns. It had entered at the back part of the thigh, and made its appearance just beneath the skin on the fore-side. As I cut on it and learned its nature, I inquired of the man how he received it — for I was impressed with the belief that it was not discharged from a Yankee gun. ' Well, sir,' said he, ' I have always been a great lover of French and American history in which the eagle figures so extensively as an emblem of freedom, and when I saw a live eagle floating and fluttering over your soldiers, yesterday, just in front of my regiment, all my old love of American freedom and loyalty returned; and shortly after, when we were obliged to run, I believed our cause was unjust, and so haunted was I with thoughts of disloyalty, and being an enemy to, and fighting against that eagle, that I determined to desert the rebel cause and come to his protection! The first opportunity I saw was this morning, when I made a rush for your lines, and was fired on by one of our men.' "

ASSAULT ON VICKSBURG.

Having chained Vicksburg on all sides with batteries by land and water, Gen. Grant ordered a combined charge to commence at 10 o'clock on the morning of the 22d of May, 1863. At the very minute the gunboats began their vengeful bombardment, McClernand on the left, McPherson in the center, and Sherman on the right with the Eagle, simultaneously moved on their columns with fixed bayonets. It was " a time that tried men's souls." The enemy burst upon the Northmen in a general pandemonium of destruction; and yet they advanced, climbing higher for the piles of the slain, treading upon their fallen companions, up furiously to "enter the lion's angry mouth." The frowning fortifications streamed forth forked lightning, blast after blast, upon our uncovered ranks below. No enemy was discernible; only solid earth works, rolling sulphurous clouds, lurid fires, missiles of death, confronted them. Must they not reach that volcano — that crater of fire, and smother it? One hour — two hours — walking over heaps of the accumulating dead and dying, and yet they struggle on; they reach the ditch; they pass it; they scale the ramparts; they plant there the Union flag; a shout goes up, but in an instant it is hushed in the throttle of death, when fresh troops come on to swell the slaughter, and yet the main works of those Southrons, so worthy of our steel, yield not an inch.

Meanwhile the Eagle clinched his claws fast to the grooves of his perch, and, standing under the proud colors, bent his head, soldier-like, on a listening angle, his fierce eyes reflecting the glare of the battle, his wings outstretched, his voice heard, as oft before, cheering his compatriots to the shock for conquest. In the general wildness and confusion, Homaston, rushing to keep at the head of the company, central in the regiment, accidentally stepped on a slippery canebrake, and fell; when, in an instant, the Eagle, shocked, doubtless, by the concussion of a bullet that glanced with a quivering pressure on his breast, mounted up with a desperate spring for a flight; but the Bearer held fast to the perch, whilst "Abe," at the other end of the cord, having gained great speed, lifted him from the ground, dragged him forward with such an impetus that it brought him abreast against a rough log, jerking back the bird and hurling them both together into the brush on the other side. The blow stunned Homaston, and "nearly knocked the breath from his body," for he lay there apparently dead, for a few moments. Whether we call it providence or not, that Eagle's flight saved the life of his Bearer. Had he not fallen at that instant, the well aimed shot of the enemy at those conspicuous standards, pouring right there in waves of fire, would have killed Homaston, and thrown the company into confusion. Lieut. Thomas B. Butler, gallantly commanding, had in the outset given Serg. Adolph Pitch special instruction to "watch the fate of Homaston," and, if he got wounded or killed, to "be sure and secure the Eagle." Seeing him fall, and noting the few moments of suspense, the Sergeant rushed toward him, just as he revived, and, finding him not killed, returned to his duty. Placing the Eagle upon his perch again, Homaston hurried forward to his post on the left of the regimental colors, borne then by Sergt. Myron Briggs, and with him, Lieut. Butler and others, stood under a large tree in front and in plain sight of the rebel batteries, not a hundred rods distant. Evidently espying the Eagle and colors, the rebels poured a special fire of grape upon the daring group, and sent a well aimed shell, which, hitting the top of the tree, cut it off, crashing to the ground, and burst with a horrid scattering, the pieces of which tore many holes in the flag, and killed several, among whom were Lieut. W. D. Chapman, of Company F, and Capt. Stephen Estee, of

Company H. The Eagle sprung for a flight again, but was held fast, and both he and his Bearer escaped unharmed. Lowering the colors and Eagle, they lay down under that shivered tree expecting annihilation, but, resolving to die at the best price, continued to fire upon the enemy, when an Adjutant rode briskly to the spot and announced the order to "go forward into the ravine, and avoid the useless slaughter." The regiment recoiled over swaths of the slain; but Butler and his company, in the dire confusion that followed, finding a perfect jam of men intercepted a passage to the right, swung over an abattis hugely piled up in sharp, threatening points; and on this they retreated a third of a mile in full sight and range of the enemy in front, firing incessantly at the dauntless boys who moved with the utmost difficulty and peril, carrying their Eagle with them safely to the ravine below. It was indeed an *eagle* leap from a maelstrom of consuming fire.

As the crowd gathered in the ravine, a soldier, chuckling over his trophy and running with the rest in high glee, brought in his hand a live rabbit which he caught in the bushes, when the whole company, forgetful of self, exclaimed — "Let's have him for Abe!" "Here, Abe!" said the sweating soldier, "you've well earned this fellow," and threw it to the perch, the Eagle catching it in his claws, and there in the raging battle, as shell and cannon were playing freely overhead, he devoured his prey, heedless of noise and excitement. How much like a soldier! His self-possessed demeanor pleased the boys vastly, it was so brave and military.

Leaving the Eagle to enjoy his meal, his Bearer took

several canteens to fill with water at a spring directly under the enemy's guns, and whilst busy at his duty, a shell fell with its thundering crash near him; one of the exploded pieces, hitting his canteen, dashed it to pieces; but, paying no attention to it, he deliberately filled the rest. "You take it cool, Ed," said a waiting boy, standing by. "Yes, cool place, this," replied Ed; "but run and see if Abe is hurt!" The pet bird was still uninjured, gorging on his rabbit. So it was everywhere; the soldiers forgot personal peril in love of the Eagle; any day the whole regiment would have fought for him. Sharing alike the dangers of march and battle, the Eagle was companion and warrior, sign and seal of victory. "Run and see if the Eagle is hurt," is the earnest expression of a soldier's undying attachment and devotion to the liberty which the noble bird so grandly emblemized.

On carefully examining "Old Abe," Homaston found he was hit probably with a spent Minie ball, and naturally concluded it occurred when he lifted him up and flung him against the log. The ball passed down his neck and breast, cutting off the feathers in its track. Had it glanced the other way, the proud bird would have fallen; but being shot in the direction of the lay of the feathers, as he faced the foe, they saved his life. Another ball passed through the web of his left wing, making a round hole in it. He is a scarred veteran to this day.

SURRENDER OF VICKSBURG.

Having foiled every strategy of the enemy to place the besiegers between the fires of Pemberton and John-

ston, our war-bird, ever as potent in battle as the ark of
Israel, flew with his peers to Young's Point, near Vicksburg. Here he was one of the "sharpshooters," under
the enemy's fire from the shore batteries. Many a poor
soldier fell; but, though constantly exposed, no harm
touched the charmed Eagle. For forty-six days, the
boys had been without tents, subject to every possible
kind of hardship and peril, without change of clothing,
and many without shoes, being feet-blistered and bleeding; and, for sixteen days, the average to a man per
day was but *one* cracker; but not a word of complaint
was uttered by a single soldier in the command.
Young's Point being a malarious locality, a large pro-
portion of the regiment was sick; but, under the skill-
ful management and fidelity of Surgeon Murta, and the
inspiriting influences of the Eagle, ever reminding
them of the holy cause for which they were suffering,
they conquered almost the pestilence. What but the
talismanic Eagle could beacon hope and triumphant
freedom amid destitution and sickness, when fiery batteries were also vomiting upon them their contents of
destruction? It was at this dangerous point that Pemberton's forces, in their mad precipitancy to escape from
Grant's coils, made their last attempt to cross the river
in flatboats; but *Eagle* eyes were on them, and when
they pushed forth on that desperate alternative, that in-
vulnerable brigade closed up the gaps with a destructive
front that drove the enemy back to his recluse. It was
like "Abe's" economical reserve of his prey for another
occasion of need; and speedily did that occasion present
itself by a flag-of-truce from Pemberton, and a meeting

with Grant under that memorable oak tree to stipulate terms of surrender, followed the next day, by the *entrée* of our army, Gen. John A. Logan at the head, with "stars and stripes," with streamers from the fleet, with martial music, with booming cannon, with a huzza which our Eagle heard and echoed in a war-scream from his post of duty, as his regiment joined its cheer in that grand jubilee which a nation at home celebrated with Te Deums of thanksgiving. We are apt to credit great victories to the Generals, but notice not the faithful privates that win them. Let us do justice, even to an Eagle. Though a private without pay, he inspired the army to health amid pestilences ; and, by his prowess, evoked unfaltering daring, that French impetuosity, that shiver of patriotic nerve which delivered the city to its rightful owners ; let our war-bird, then, be mentioned in history as the inaugural of that eventful celebration on the 4th of July, 1863.

"UNVEXED TO THE SEA."

With an acumen characteristic of the American mind, the Congress of the Southern Confederacy foresaw, that a possession of the Lower Mississippi would be virtually the establishment of a separate government; and with a wonderful alacrity was a policy, aiming at this result, executed early in the war by fortifying the high bluffs of both shores at the most commanding and impregnable points to prevent northern navigation, and by organizing a land force sufficient to baffle a Federal attempt to break the blockade. When the Union army entered upon its conquest, the Confederacy held the

country from Columbus down to New Orleans. To
open the Mississippi was the problem. The rivals were
of equal bravery; the difference was in the righteousness
of the cause. Of the strategical movements it is need-
less to speak here, save that, when the fleet of Farragut,
conquering the mouth of the river, reducing New Orleans to order under Benj. F. Butler, combined with the
fleet of Foote, moving down the river from the North,
both backed by their " three hundred thousand more,"
under the leadership of such men as Banks, Pope, Mc-
Clernand, McPherson, Logan, Stanley, Blair, Washburn,
Buell, Mitchell, and others of like calibre, — when the
northern wing, after several experiments, at length
gained the rear of Vicksburg, under the command of
Maj. Gen. Grant, subduing the city by a deliberate
siege, necessarily followed by the surrender of Port
Hudson to Gen. Banks, only four days after, — then the
" Father of Waters," blockaded and chained by rebel
batteries for more than two years, " ran unvexed to the
sea; " then this " possession of America," that deprived
the enemy of sustenance from the west, became the
initial of Sherman's Great March to the Atlantic, which
bisected the Confederacy east and west, leaving the invincible Grant the honor of finishing the rebellion in
Richmond. Thus our emblem-warrior of the dark wing
— " Old Abe " — was a conspicuous actor in the most
gigantic and far reaching strategy of generalship ever
known in military annals; and in it all, moving with
his column in every possible direction, unconscious of
this magnificent design, he was hailed as the swift messenger of justice by all that proud and victorious army.

The triumph of our arms was purchased at the cost of "the flower of the North," at the cost of brave hearts in the sunny South — though misguided — till our mutual weeping rose to Heaven for mercy; but, as our lamented Lincoln said on the battle-field of Gettysburg,—

"From these honored dead take increased devotion to the cause for which they gave the last full measure of devotion, and their high resolve, that the dead shall not have died in vain; that the nation shall, under God, have a new birth of freedom, and that the government of the people, by the people, and for the people, shall not perish from the earth."

CHASTISING THE ILLINOIS SOLDIER.

While "Old Abe's" regiment was stationed at Messenger's Ford, the latter part of July, there protecting property and life against guerilla hordes, a squad of the 93d Illinois came one day purposely to see the Eagle. Having heard of his dislike of strangers, one of them was quite shy, careful not to approach within the length of his cord; but the boys of the Eighth, ever on the alert for fun, importuned him to throw up his cap and " see how nice the Eagle will catch it." The plumaged patriot was then in a tree surveying his guests with severe scrutiny. Up went the cap, when "Abe," catching it with his claws, glanced down at the soldier with a roguish whistle, and trampled it under his feet, hovering and rustling his wings, and then holding it there, tore it up with his beak, flinging the shreds down with a disdainful — " How do you like to insult an Eagle, sir? " Soon after this incident, while "Abe " was on his perch surveying the trappings of war, a negro passed under him very carelessly, when, quick as a dart, he reached down and snatched off the grimacing darkie's cap, tore it up, chuckling over the ruins. He wished to teach the negro, whom he came to emancipate, a proper deference to superiors.

"TAKING A GLASS!"

"Old Abe's" honor was not always at par. A few days after, while the regiment was on picket guard at Bear Creek, he followed the example of certain dignitaries of the army — got drunk! A soldier, having bought some peach brandy, poured out a saucerful, left it a few moments on the ground, and turned to attend to some camp duty, when "Abe," always on the watch for spoils, "took a glass," and, in a little while, was intoxicated after the usual style of hard drinkers. He lolled his head and tried to vomit, flapped his wings heavily upon the ground, rolled over, and behaved in an unbecoming manner for an Eagle!

RED RIVER EXPEDITION.

In September, Mr. Homaston resigned his responsible office, when the gallant Lieut. Butler, then commanding, conferred the honor upon John Buckhardt, of Eau Claire, who was initiated into the military art of bearing the Eagle in McPherson's and Logan's victorious charge upon the enemy at Brownsville, October 14, 1863.

After various oscillating marches in every important movement of the campaign, "Abe" was next seen proudly marching with Gen. Sherman's army, on the 27th of February, 1864, into Central Mississippi, as the Roman heraldry of success. Arriving at Canton, his regiment was suddenly ordered back to Vicksburg to guard it against its being retaken by the enemy. It was a precipitate march on foot of one hundred and fourteen miles, in seventy hours, with the swiftness of an Eagle in pursuit of the hawk. Pestilence, fatigue, hunger, battle, had depleted the ranks. The loyal bird missed familiar companions at almost every adventure; yet his spirit was unconquerable like that of his compatriots. At Vicksburg, fresh recruits awoke new vigor. It is said "Old Abe" actually manifested a decided pleasure while scanning the men on dress parade. Soldierly in his instincts, he seemed to understand that the war was to be carried to the bitter end — to the last dying gasp of an enslaving rebellion.

That army had conquered the Mississippi, but one of its main arteries — Red River — remained blockaded by the enemy. Should the "Eagles" advance, or have a furlough to which they were entitled? "Country first!" said all; "every tributary even shall be restored!" Such was "Old Abe's" vote, if there were anything significant of consent in his warlike aspect. Under command of Gen. A. J. Smith, they embarked on transports, the 10th of March, 1864, with a force of 20,000, accompanied by Admiral Porter's fleet, down the Mississippi, up the Red River, up the Atchafalaya, to Simmsport, Louisiana, where a portion of the troops landed, marching four miles to Fort Scurry, situated at the junction of Yellow Bayou with Bayou de Glaise, and struck an effectual blow at the enemy — the Eighth being in the advance with their invincible Eagle. Following the Bayou de Glaise, on the 14th, they marched

over a charming country and were greeted with joy by
the French or Creole people. As they displayed white
flags and waved their handkerchiefs, "Old Abe," accus-
tomed mainly to menacing or scornful attitudes from
the Southern populace, eyed their demonstrations with
his sharp eyes without a response, as if to say, "Who
knows whether you are loyal?" But, when his regiment cheered, he lustily flapped his wings. Advancing
to Fort de Russy on the Red River — which the spring
before destroyed our fine iron-clad "Queen of the
West"— they immediately invested it, on the 15th, and,
by assault, carried it in twenty minutes, with the Eagle-
scream heard upon the ramparts. Here, joined by the
fleet, they proceeded the next morning up the river,
fifty miles, to Alexandria, where a request was made by
several regimental officers and captains for company C
to transfer the Eagle to the regiment. "He is a national bird," was the argument, "and should be regimental."
Quite an animated disputation ensued, ending in a written statement of the original claims of the company,
which was sent to Gen. Mower, who decided in favor of
the company as the lawful owner.

YANKEE TRICK.

While waiting the arrival of Gen. Banks at Alexandria, the "Eagles," in the second brigade under Gen.
Mower, "marched, on the 21st, along Bayou Rapide,
over very muddy roads, a distance of twenty miles, to
Henderson's Hill, where the enemy was discovered in
strong position, defended by artillery" (see Adj. Gaylord's Report for 1864, p. 36). Finding it impractical

to attack the enemy in front, the brigade made a detour of fifteen miles, through cane swamps, where the enemy supposed a passage could not be effected. It was then midnight, and "dark as Erebus." Stealthily they moved. Quick—a single note of the Eagle's whistle—it was a sign, "Be on the guard!" What was it? A step approached. It was a courier from the rebel fort, bearing dispatches from the commander to Gen. Dick Taylor, then only four miles distant with a force of 12,000 strong, asking for reënforcements to "repulse the Yankees in front." The man, supposing at first in the darkness that he was with Confederate soldiers, divulged the rebel countersign. He was captured and forced to lead the "Eagle army" into the fort by the talisman of that countersign — the very dark our Providence, — when three hundred and fifty strong, with four guns, four hundred horses, and a supply of ammunition and stores, were captured. It was a descent of the American Eagle upon his prey; the rebels cursed and swore at the "Yankee trick," as "Abe" screamed his war-cry of victory.

Returning the next day to Alexandria, the "Eagles" were in motion again on the 26th, traveling thirty-three miles on Red River to Cotile, where they made a junction with Gen. Banks' army, and, on the 2d of April, embarking on transports, found the enemy, eighty miles farther up, in force at Grand Ecore. Here another question of dispute arose as to what company should carry the Eagle, for company C was assigned the post of Provost Guard at Division Head Quarters. It was finally tendered Company I, with the regimental colors — the only instance when he was out of the hands of company C during the whole war — and carried by Mr. Buckhardt through all the rest of that expedition.

COVERING THE RETREAT.

It is a remarkable fact, that even in retreat, when hard pressed by the enemy, that part of the army in which the Eagle fought with his braves by his screams and furious wings, was also irresistible in a contesting battle. At Grand Ecore, Gen. Banks' army commenced its more vigorous operations. Detachments of the Eighth were deployed as skirmishers, the rebels retiring with slight show of resistance, as if to lead into their jaws of destruction.

"At this time the river was rapidly falling, endangering their communications, and Gen. Banks' army having passed on in advance towards Pleasant Hill and Mansfield, for Shreveport, Gen. Smith's forces [Eagle Corps] marched in the same direction, on the morning of the 7th, and having toiled upwards of thirty miles through rain and over horrible roads, arrived on the following day at Pleasant Hill. During the early part of the day, a portion of Gen. Banks' army had been defeated at Sabine Cross Roads, and driven back in the direction of Pleasant Hill; when Gen. Smith's army was at once placed in position to rally our retreating forces, and check the advance of the enemy, who attacked our lines vigorously, on the 9th, and after a severe contest, lasting four hours, was repulsed at all points, and driven from the field. The Eighth, having been posted to prevent a flank movement of the enemy, was double-quicked to the front, and joined in the pursuit. After the battle, a retreat was ordered, and the army returned, on the 11th, to Grand Ecore."—*Adjutant General's Report, 1864.*"

"If we must retreat, let it be a victory," seemed to be "Old Abe's" motto; and "No surrender!" was his watchword; and well did he illustrate it during the remainder of the retreat. As his compatriots fired back, now on a rush, now on the deliberate aim, now flying to gain a shelter of defense, our Eagle, furious and on fire, scanned friend and foe through the chinks of the curling smoke, cheering his own with the splendor of his example. It was but to look at that Eagle, raised aloft, with wings flapping, with eyes of lightning, with voice like the Indian warwhoop, and know that the augury was hopeful and their cause was just. This rendered them unconquerable even in disaster. Covering the retreat for a distance of eighty miles, they held a bridge against the enemy, on the 24th, at Nachitoches; in the evening of the same day they fought him at Clouterville, driving him back in confusion, as the army made further advance in that retreat. Day and night, our Eagle was on the march and battle, the inspiriting and unfaltering messenger of the invincible Eighth, that saved Gen. Banks' army from utter rout, till safely arrived at Alexandria, on the 26th, subsisting on short rations, weary, repulsed in the main, but not disheartened. The evacuation of Red River being now determined upon, the "Eagle-wing of the Army," under Gen. Smith, moved up Bayou Rapide, "Old Abe" on his heraldic post, to check the enemy during the construction of the celebrated dam, by which, through the engineering skill of Col. Bailey, of the 4th Wisconsin, our fleet was saved. On the 3d of May, the Eagle was with his skirmishers, covering the front of the army from Bayou Roberts to Bayou La Moore, constantly under fire till the 13th, when the

retreat of our whole army was resumed. On the left
of the retreating column could be seen our Northern
Eagle of tireless wing, turning, backward wheeling,
advancing, almost shooting the enemy with those
war-lit eyes; and, as his braves fought on, over all those
weary miles, back to Fort de Russy, resting only two
hours there, on to the battle of Maysville, to the battle
of Mansura, to the battle at Calhoun's Plantation, to
the battle at Bayou de Glaise, to the battle at Atchafalaya, he was indeed a veteran soldier in example of
fortitude and daring, ever the sign above the heads of
the moving columns of the eventual triumph of our
arms. Crossing the Atchafalaya, pressing to the mouth
of that river, on the 21st, our unconquered Eagle was
at last safe with the surviving members of his regiment
on board a transport, landing at Vicksburg, on the 24th.
Learning that the enemy, inflated at their seeming success, was attempting to blockade the Mississippi again,
the regiment and "Old Abe" rushed with other forces
to Lake Chicot, and, on the 6th of June, blasted the
design, and left the river in its "free course to run and
be glorified." The gallant Col. J. W. Jefferson said, in
his report to Gov. Lewis, of this continuous battle of
twenty-seven days:

"Half the time my men have been on short rations, and
no opportunity of getting clothing for them in the past
three months. My noble soldiers are barefooted and in rags,
nevertheless the health and efficiency of the men were never
better. The campaign is a failure, but in every instance that
our army (Smith's) has had occasion to fight the enemy, we
have whipped him and driven him in disorder. The regiment
has been first to the front and last to leave it."

CHAPTER III.

CENTENNIAL BIRD OF STATE.

"With malice toward none, with charity for all, with firmness in the right, as God gives us to see the right, let us strive on to finish the work we are in, to bind up the nation's wounds, and care for him who shall have borne the battle, and for his widow and his orphans; to do all which may achieve and cherish a just and lasting peace among ourselves and with all nations." — ABRAHAM LINCOLN's INAUGURAL OF 1865.

YEARS of war — three of them — oh, how terrible to endure! and yet the Union was not saved; there was a more urgent call than ever for recruits, and not in vain was the call for re-enlistment. They were patriots. They would blush with shame to delay the ægis of peace. Noble soldiers! Up to June, 1864, six hundred and thirty-one were able to do duty. About three hundred of these re-enlisted, each having a furlough of thirty days. By battles and diseases, two hundred had gone down to patriot graves. But what joy in the hearts of those living veterans as they thought of home — what joy admixed with sorrow as they contemplated their country's redemption from tyranny, purchased at so dear a price!

On the 19th of June, 1864, those war-scarred veterans, with their renowned Eagle, left Memphis and arrived at Chicago on the 21st, welcomed at the Soldiers' Rest.

"The ramparts are all filled with men and women,
  With peaceful men and women, that send onwards
  Kisses and welcoming upon the air
  Which they make breezy with affectionate gestures.
  From all the joyous towers ring out the merry bells,
  The joyous vespers of a bloody day.
  O happy man! O fortunate! for whom
  The well-known door, the faithful arms are open,
  The faithful, tender arms, with mute embracing."

The State authorities in Madison received a telegram
from Chicago, stating that the Eighth Wisconsin Veterans, numbering two hundred and forty strong, would
arrive at that city on the 22d. They were received with
a most cordial welcome. The Madison *State Journal*,
of the 23d, thus sums up the imposing scene:

"The reënlisted veterans of the 8th Wisconsin regiment arrived
on the afternoon train, Tuesday, and after a good dinner prepared
for them at Mosher's Railroad House, marched up town to the
Capitol Park, where the reception took place a little after six
o'clock. A large concourse of citizens had assembled to witness
the spectacle. Flags were displayed along the streets, the bells
of the city rung, and a national salute fired.

"The live Eagle, 'Old Abe,' and the tattered and riddled colors
of the regiment attracted all eyes. Since we first saw him at
Camp Randall, in 1861, 'Old Abe' has grown considerably, and
has acquired dignity and ease of bearing. He sits on his perch
undisturbed by any noise or tumult, the impersonation of
haughty defiance. He has shared all the long marches of this
regiment, including Sherman's great raid and the compaign up
Red River, and passed through a great number of battles, in
which he has once or twice had some of his feathers shot away,
but has never received a scratch from a rebel bullet sufficient to
draw blood. He is the pet of the whole regiment."

After the regiment had been drawn up in the Park,
Gov. Lewis being then absent, the soldiers were elo-

quently addressed by Gen. Lucius Fairchild, Hon. J. H. Carpenter, Hon. Chauncey Abbott and Adj. Gen. Augustus Gaylord.

Nor was our Eagle forgotten in the general hilarity. An object of majestic interest, well had he fulfilled the augury of victory, three years before heralded in that city:

"We welcome your Eagle, that National emblem, whose fame has been widely spread and become historic through pen and song. I have often wondered what sensations must have filled the mind of rebels as you have borne him proudly with your regiment, and while they remember the present attitude they maintain toward our government, one would think that the very sight would cause them to hide their heads in shame. Bear him ever aloft with your advancing shout, and let the rebels remember — yes, *teach* them that —

> ' Ne'er shall the rage of the conflict be o'er,
> And ne'er shall the warm blood of life cease to flow,
> And still 'mid the smoke of the battle shall soar,
> Our Eagle — till scattered and fled be the foe.'

"At the conclusion of Gen. Fairchild's remarks, Col. Jefferson briefly responded, returning the thanks of the regiment for the cordial welcome that had been extended to them, and proposed 'three cheers and a big Eagle' for the Union, the President of the United States, and the State officers of Wisconsin. Three cheers were given with great enthusiasm by the boys of the Eighth, the Eagle evidently understanding his part, and at the third hurrah, stretching himself to his full height, and expanding his wings to the utmost."

RETURN TO EAU CLAIRE.

Early on the morning of Sunday, June 26, a remnant of company C with "Old Abe" arrived at Eau Claire, and was greeted with booming cannon, martial music, patriotic songs, and an abundant feast. It was a greeting of civilian and soldier, a welcome of gratitude, a kindling of the memories of the heroic dead, a rejuvenation of hope to our bleeding country. The Eagle, assigned a spacious yard under a shading oak, received his old acquaintances with his usual dignity — so much dignity, that scarcely any one dared to touch even a kingly feather. How had he honored his native State! How proud were the Eau Clairians of that monarch bird! The Eau Claire *Free Press* thus speaks of those soldiers and their Eagle :

" It will be remembered, that nearly three years ago, a band of the stalwart sons of Wisconsin, numbering one hundred strong, under command of Capt. J. E. Perkins — who fell while gallantly leading his men in the battle of Farmington, Miss.— left their homes in the Chippewa Valley, and all that was dear to them, and joined the Eighth regiment at Madison, to defend our nation from the grasp of rebellion. A couch upon the tented field, the hardship and dangers of battle, the diseases incident to camp life, were willingly accepted for the sake of country. They swore that they would defend our national banner to the last drop of their blood; and they have kept that oath.

"The company has been filled up several times, and now only fifty-six are left of the gallant band. Excepting the few discharged, the rest are numbered with the honored dead. Thirty have reënlisted, thinking their services are as much needed now as when the rebellion first broke out. All honor is due them for their patriotism. They bring with them the 'Eagle,' whence the regiment derives its name.

*　　*　　"The brave old Eighth has withstood the repeated charges of rebel infantry, the daring dashes of their cavalry, the galling fire of their musketry—*never flinching*. The Eagle is returned to us unharmed. Well may Eau Claire be proud.— proud that she has a representative company in the Eagle Regiment— proud that the Eagle, so famous, is a native of the Chippewa Valley."　　　　　　　　*

CELEBRATION AT CHIPPEWA FALLS.

In a few days "Old Abe" visited his own county — Chippewa — where he heard again the mellow flow of the waters that kiss the ferns of his wild home, caught with fiery glances the sunlight that dusts with gold the lakes where "Chief Sky" snatched from his eyrie our plumaged hero and gave him to the "pale-face," as if to indicate an equal claim to a protective freedom thus emblemized to his "sable brother." On the 4th of July, 1864, the Union people celebrated our Day of Independence at Chippewa Falls. Several soldiers with "Old Abe" were present. A huge wigwam was constructed, in which was served a great feast, the proceeds being for our suffering soldiers. Headed by a band of music and the Eagle on his old perch, followed by his compatriots in arms, the enthusiastic procession marched through the streets; it was inspiring. A correspondent, writing about it, says:

"The boys of the Eighth, with their pet bird, honored the stand. The dignified and noble looking creature remained quiet until Mr. Barrett addressed the veterans and their Eagle, when he, (the Eagle), turned his head with admirable grace, and with a most intelligent expression in his eyes, listened attentively to the peroration, and, when it was finished, with his beak he smoothed down the feathers of his breast, manifesting great pride at the attention bestowed upon him. At the close of the speech, three cheers were given for the old starry flag, three for the brave boys of the Eighth, and three for the War-Eagle, and instantly that Eagle, catching the enthusiasm, rose upon his perch, flapped his wings, and with a look expressive of delight, uttered a sharp, shrill cry, calling forth the applause of the excited multitude."

6

"OLD ABE" A GENTLEMAN PASSENGER.

Furlough days having expired, the regiment on different routes hurried back to Memphis, about the first of August. It will be remembered that about that time a Union patriot did not calculate courtesy to our country's enemy against principle; that the bravery of a soldier rose to audacity, when the occasion warranted it. Confident of "Old Abe's" rights, Mr. Buckhardt took him on board a passenger car of the Illinois Central Railroad, amid the stare and cheer of hundreds. The conductor soon appeared, and seeing the bird occupying half a seat, demanded double fare. The Bearer refusing to pay only for himself, high words ensued with considerable swearing.

"Pay for that thing, or I'll put you out!" again muttered the enraged conductor, placing his hand with heavy force upon the Bearer's shoulder.

"Te Eakel is von free pirdt — free 'Merigan Eakel; — he ride free."

Matters grew squally; the conductor seized him by the collar, when, with a rush and a menace, several soldiers circled around John and his Eagle, demanding "fair play for 'Old Abe.'" Seeing this unlooked for motion, and realizing the fact that nearly all the passengers sympathized with the German, the conductor, showed his valor by sliding backwards with an adroit expertness out into another car.

"Copperhead !" shouted the boys with a laugh; "might as well fight such *sneaks* as rebs, John, eh?" The result was the soldier-bird rode the entire route as a "gentlemen passenger," much to the satisfaction and amusement of the Union friends on board.

BALD HEADED VETERAN.

Soldiers left at Memphis could scarcely recognize "Old Abe," he had changed so by his northern trip. In fact he had become white headed; so they called him "Bald Headed Veteran." Indian traders say the head and neck feathers of this species of eagle, for the first three and four years, are dark, after which they gradually turn to white. This agrees with the fact stated of "Old Abe," for at the time of his furlough, he was between three and four years old.

Maria S. Cummings, in the October number of "Our Young Folks," for 1866, giving an outline of "Old Abe's" career, draws the following beautiful moral about what she styles "Our Bald Headed Representative:"

"He belongs to the Bald-Head, or more correctly the White-Headed family, a species that in some respects are all young veterans, inasmuch as, at three or four years old, their head-feathers which were originally brown, have become snowy white, giving them a dignified and venerable appearance. The other name of Bald-Head is derived from a spot between the beak and eyes, which is almost wholly destitute of feathers, so that the Bald Eagle, which is the emblem of America, assumes in his youth the honors which belong to a bald head and a hoary crown, although one would think he might afford to wait longer for them, as the eagle is a very long-lived bird, instances having been known of his living to be a hundred years old.

"And so with the country of which the Bald-Head is the representative. Although America is a young nation, she has had so much experience, and has progressed so much faster than the nations of the Old World, that, if she could see herself in the mirror of history, she would appear with a fresh, ruddy face, and a strong frame, but a little wrinkled and bald about the temples, and with hair which care and anxiety have turned prematurely gray. But long life to her, and a high place among the nations! and if she too has become a veteran in her youth, may it be with her as with our Eagle, — only the courage, strength, and wisdom which she has acquired on her many hard-fought fields that entitle her to the name."

"OLD ABE'S" LAST BATTLE.

Rallying again around the flag and the Eagle, in Gen. A. J. Smith's division, there was a rush, August 13th, 1864, after Forrest and his hosts. Crossing the Tallahatchie River, and skirmishing near Abbeville — "Old Abe," on his war-shield, carried by Mr. Buckhardt — the Union army met the enemy at Hurricane Creek, Miss. Having two batteries on a distant eminence, to back his advance, Gen. Joseph Mower, who had so long distinguished himself, led his faithful brigade within a mile of the hill that peered up a hundred feet above the open field. The batteries of the rival forces played upon each other until night, when, under its cover, our cavalry by an expert movement, flanked the rebel lines on both sides, leaving the front open for a charge. On they rushed, intercepted by a muddy creek, and thick clump of alders, but forming on the other side, the steady columns moved like a tornado, the "Eagles," wheeling to the back of the hill, when "Old Abe," again in all his glory, with eye of lightning, with head and neck elongated to swiftest dash, with a whistle quick and startling to nerve and pluck, charged with them up, up the ramparts, flinging the enemy off as with the sweep of an Eagle's wing, frightened, dismayed, broken, narrowly escaping at a fearful loss. As the dead and wounded lay side by side — brothers there, as by right they should be, at the portal of death — the very ground trembled for the shout of the victors, while the scream of the war-bird was heard clear and distinct amid the general carnival of groans and rejoicings.

This was "Old Abe's" last battle in the Great Rebellion. It was the seal of his perpetual conquests. He was the hero of about twenty-five great battles, and as many skirmishes. To what agency must we attribute his "charmed life," when the story must be told again and again by patriot sires to their worthy sons, that, though in the fiercest fights, not a Bearer of the colors or of the Eagle — ever conspicuous marks for the enemy — was shot down. The Eagle seemed as protective to these Bearers as was the standard of the cross in the battles of Constantine. In the great battle against Lucinius, which gave Constantine the undivided mastery of the Roman world, one man, who, in terror, transferred the standard to another, was immediately pierced by a spear, while the Bearer of it passed on unhurt amid a shower of javelins, and not a man in its immediate neighborhood was even wounded. If the Eagle could dodge bullets, as the soldiers declare he did, not so the Bearers. Many a sharpshooter fired at these boys, but failed to kill one of them. In the bloodiest carnage, they and their living standard were unharmed. Did it not portend the preservation of the Union? a Providence, holding death at bay, as with our Washington, when British soldiers singled him out, to prove that the American Eagle of Justice can never fall at the hands of an enemy?

"OLD ABE'S" BATTLES AND SKIRMISHES.

Fredericktown, Mo.,	Oct. 21,	1861
Siege of New Madrid and Island No 10, Mo.,	M'h and Ap,	1862
Point Pleasant, Mo.,	M'ch 20,	1862
Farmington, Miss.,	May 9,	1862
Before Corinth, Miss.,	May 28,	1862
Iuka, Miss.,	Sept. 12,	1862
Burnsville, Miss.,	Sept. 13,	1862
Iuka, Miss.,	Sept. 16, 18,	1862
Corinth, Miss.,	Oct. 3, 4,	1862
Tallahatchie, Miss.,	Dec. 2,	1862
Mississippi Springs, Miss.,	May 13,	1863
Jackson, Miss.,	May 14,	1863
Assault on Vicksburg, Miss.,	May 22,	1863
Mechanicsburg, Miss.,	June 4,	1863
Richmond, La.,	June 15,	1863
Vicksburg, Miss.,	June 24,	1863
Surrender of Vicksburg, Miss.,	July 4,	1863
Brownsville, Miss.,	Oct. 14,	1863
Fort Scurry, La.,	M'ch 13,	1864
Fort de Russy, La.,	M'ch 15,	1864
Henderson's Hill, La.,	M'ch 15,	1864
Grand Ecore, La.,	Apr. 2,	1864
Pleasant Hill, La.,	Apr. 8, 9,	1864
Nachitoches, La.,	Apr. 20,	1864
Kane River, La.,	Apr. 22,	1864
Clouterville and Crane Hill, La.,	Apr. 23,	1864
Bayou Rapide, La.,	May 2,	1864
Bayou La Moore, La.,	May 3,	1864
Bayou Roberts, La.,	May 4-6,	1864
Moore's Plantation, La.,	May 8-12,	1864
Mansura, La.,	May 16,	1864
Maysville, La.,	May 17,	1864
Calhoun's Plantation, La.,	May 18,	1864
Bayou de Glaise, La.,	May 18,	1864
Lake Chicot, La.,	June 6,	1864
Hurricane Creek, La.,	Aug. 13,	1864

WAR BEARERS OF THE EAGLE.

1. James McGennis, of Eau Claire, from Sept. 1, 1861, to May 30, 1862.
2. Thos. J. Hill, of Eau Claire, from May 30, 1862, to Aug. 18, 1862.
3. David McLane, of Menomonie, from Aug. 18, 1862, to Oct. —, 1862.
4. Edward Homaston, of Eau Claire, from Oct. —, 1862, to Sept. —, 1863.
5. John Buckhardt, of Eau Claire, from Sept. —, 1863, to Sept. —, 1864.
5. John F. Hill, during transit from Chicago to Madison, Sept., —, 1864.

MUSTERED OUT.

Returning to Memphis, on the 29th, in pursuit of Forrest, who was then fighting the patriotic Gen. C. C. Washburn, "Old Abe" parted with the regiment for the last time. Having served the three years' enlistment, a portion of Company C was to be mustered out. Now the serious question arose, "What shall be done with the Soldier-Bird?" A discussion followed. Some were in favor of giving him to the County of Eau Claire, others to the National Government at Washington, others to the State of Wisconsin. All things considered, the latter motion prevailed, and was finally voted unanimously. It was an affectionate adieu to their "companion in arms." The main body of that veteran regiment remained till the close of the war, fighting other battles, under gallant officers whose record is unsullied, campaigning in eleven states, traveling by rail, river, and on foot, 15,179 miles, and was mustered out at Demopolis, Ala., Sept. 5, 1865, crowned with palms of victory, blessed by a grateful country.

Twenty-six of Company C took their precious charge — " Old Abe " — and wended their way north, reaching Chicago, Sept. 21, 1864, where Buckhardt resigned his " Eagle Commission " to John F. Hill, brother of Thomas. Being disabled from a wound received at Corinth, he was obliged to rest occasionally at the corners of the streets, where knots of citizens gathered to learn of the career of the Eagle. He was returning from the war with the proudest and most famous bird that ever fanned the breeze of heaven. The " Eagle-Veteran " of the Great Rebellion, with eye unblanched, with fearless and untiring wing, with talons still grasping the lightnings of battle, comes home to rest, crowned with honors. Oft had he by example cheered the desponding, roused ambition, and encouraged sacrifices. He had enlivened the dull hours of camp life, and stood aloft with unfurled pinions, and with wild, terrible shriek, led the deadly charge to victory. Under the war-flag, tattered and torn, yet blazing with the stars he loved, this " Bird of the Union " had taught by his spirit the true art of conquest, and evoked a purpose, a daring, a martyr spirit, that can be felt only in like hearts that love liberty better than life, that gives us the cross and the future the crown.

TRANSFERRED TO THE STATE.

Arriving at Madison, on the 22d of Sept., 1864, those war-scarred soldiers were paid for their services; and now the Eagle must have attention. The hero-bird, on his old perch, was taken across the shady park and thence into the aisle of the Capitol, where Capt. Wolf and Mr. Hill, with a few other soldiers, were met by Quarter Master Gen. N. F. Lund, who immediately entered the Executive Department and informed Gov. Lewis that "Old Abe" was in waiting. The Madison *State Journal* thus described the event:

"An interesting presentation was made at 3 o'clock yesterday (the 26'h) afternoon, in the Governor's room. This was nothing less than the presentation of the celebrated Eagle of the 8th Regiment to the State of Wisconsin. Capt. Wolf, of Company C, the color company, and the one having the care of the Eagle, presented it to Gov. Lewis, stating how it was valued by the regiment; how it had been in their midst, between their flags in many a victorious conflict with the enemy, and how it had cheered and kept up their spirits by its bright eye and dauntless mien during weary marches and the tedium of camp life. It had been with them for three years; and when the time of the men of the company expired, and they were about to leave the service, they and the veterans voted that the Eagle should be presented to the State, to be kept as an honored and inspiring memento of the 8th Regiment, and the times in which it had fought the battles of the nation with the true and strong men who rallied around the flag.

"Gov. Lewis, on the part of the State, had pleasure in accepting the famous Eagle of the 8th regiment, and assured the Captain, that it would be well cared for at the Capitol, where it would remain to invoke inspiring memories of the brave boys who had carried it with such honor to themselves and the State.

"The Governor then handed the Eagle on its perch to Quartermaster General Lund, who said he would see that it was suitably kept.

"The Eagle never looked better than at present, its plumage being full and glossy and its eye piercingly bright. It will be an honored curiosity at the Capitol, and the many tales connected with its service in the field with the gallant 8th, will often be told and re-told to the admiring crowds that perhaps for years and years will come to see the Badger Eagle."

The following is a copy of the receipt of the Eagle from Gov. Lewis to Gen. Lund:

"MADISON, *Sept.* 26, 1864.

"Received from the Governor, the live Eagle, 'Old Abe' of the Eighth Reg't Wis. Vol. Infantry.

"The Eagle was formally presented to the Governor, in his office, to-day at 3 o'clock, by Capt. Victor Wolf, of company C, in behalf of the company and the regiment, the above named company having brought the Eagle into Camp Randall, in September, 1861, from Eau Claire, and carried him through all the marches and battles of the regiment since that time. This having been the color company, the Eagle has been borne by them beside the colors of the regiment. The majority of the company had within the past three days been paid off and mustered out of service. They arrived here on the 22d inst. In presenting the Eagle to the Governor, Capt. Wolf said he had been a good soldier, and never had flinched in battle or march; that he had been well cared for by company C, and he hoped he would be as well taken care of by the State. In reply, the Governor assured the Captain that the Eagle should be well and carefully taken care of, and as safely kept as possible, as long as he lived."

Gen. Lund and Adj't Gen. Gaylord, in their annual reports for 1864, speaking of the old flags of the regiments returned to the State — "torn and shattered by shot and shell, often all that remained of them being a few 'honorable rags'"— classifies "Old Abe" with the War Relics. (Adj't Gen. Report, pp. 146, 422.)

The State authorities and citizens of Madison at large, are much attached to "Old Abe," and often inquire how he fares. Like any other illustrious veteran, he is brought out and paraded on occasions of public military exercises or review, and is always sure to excite attention and enthusiasm. Even now, at his quiet home in Madison, under the shadow of the Capitol, this brave bird is much excited by the report of firearms, flapping his wings and otherwise manifesting his familiarity with their use. At present he has a pleasant and well-lighted room in the basement of the Capitol, in which is a permanent roost; he also has the freedom of an adjoining room, and, in the summer, the Capitol Park is his, under the care of his attendant.

"OLD ABE'S" FIGHT WITH "ANDY JOHNSON."

A few years ago, "Abe" had an eagle-mate from the Rocky Mountains, that came into the possession of the 49th Wisconsin Regiment, near the close of the war, and subsequently was given to the State. This "vicious bird," as he was called, bore the honored name of "Phil Sheridan," but it was afterwards changed to "Andy Johnson." Whenever these eagles met, there was sure to be a terrible battle of wings, beaks and claws, "holding on like bull dogs," each intent on the mastery. It was always necessary to part the "Chippewa and Rocky Mountain Eagles," to prevent their injuring each other in those desperate fights. One day, "Old Abe" being somewhat unwell, was fairly whipped by his antagonist. Laying up a store of vengeance, subsequently "Abe," with a cunning instinct flew upon the top of the open door, and when, at last, "Andy" appeared, he descended upon him with a loud scream, and fastened his claws in the neck of his enemy and completely vanquished him. "Andy" soon after pined, and died in the spring of 1874 — doubtless from the effects of "Abe's" talons — when his skin was properly stuffed and is kept, as a relic of the war, in the Historical Rooms. The victo-

rious Chippewa Eagle showed no whimpering over the
demise, but seemed to glory in at last being sole monarch of the "Eagle Department of State."

COMPANIONSHIP OF "OLD ABE."

Since the war "Old Abe" has had many to care for
him. First, John H. McFarland, State Armorer, suc-
ceeeded by Capt. A. R. McDonald, during Gov. Fairchild's, Washburn's and part of Taylor's administra-
tion; subsequently by Capt. John Stock and E. G. Lin-
derman, present State Armorer. Being a military character and public property, he belongs in the Department of the Adjutant General, now filled by Gen. Geo.
A. Hanaford, who takes a great pride in the war-bird.
Wm. J. Jones, Hugh Lewis, Eugene Bowen, Geo. W.
Baker — each of whom has the honor of an "armless
sleeve " — Harry W. Lovejoy, another "scarred veteran,"
Thomas Welch and I. E. Troan have had more or less
charge over him.

Bearers and attendants have invariably cherished a
strong affection for "Old Abe." There is that about
him which always engenders a deep and lasting friendship. So intelligent and grateful for fidelity to his
needs, so keenly just, he is indeed the most winning
warrior that ever fought a battle. Capt. McDonald,
who was uncommonly successful in managing his "Eagle Highness," had him so well trained that if any one
entered the "Eagle Department" whom the Captain did
not want there, a look and word to "Old Abe" were
sufficient hints for him to drive such out with a furious
onslaught. The bird knew even his master's step, and

would cheer and chuckle before he opened the door. He is good company all the live-long day. Occasionally, when the Captain put a gun in a vice to repair it, "Abe" would hop on to the other end, intently watching the process, and if his master dropped his hammer, down would jump the Eagle, pick it up and run off with it for a mutual frolic. When specially invited, he would carefully walk up the Captain's arm, and, standing upon his shoulder, affectionately rub his white head against his master's face and comb his beard with his beak, ever whistling a merry appreciation of such confidence and companionable attention.

Though a bird of prey, of merciless reputation, he has sometimes exhibited wonderful forbearance and even friendship for his victim. After the war, a beautiful red rooster was given to him for a dinner, and not only did he spare the creature's life, but became his fast friend, both playing and roosting together on the same perch.

His memory is as keen as his friendship. After the war, Edward Homaston chanced to see the Eagle in a crowd at the depot in Madison. He knew his bird, but feigning otherwise, he exclaimed, "Why, here is an Eagle!" and instantly put out his hand to pat him on the head, when his attendant checked him, saying, "Take care, there, the Eagle will hurt you!" "Hurt me?" said Homaston, almost embracing "Old Abe." "See here, man!" It was a beautiful sight, indeed; the Eagle extended his wings, screeched and cooed, overjoyed at once more greeting his old Bearer. A similar recognition occurred sometime in the year of 1867, in the Eagle's apartment in the Capitol, as related by Mrs. Ole Bull. This lady, and some friends, were visiting "Old Abe," careful not to approach too near, when a gentleman, whom they afterwards learned was one of the Bearers while in active service, entered the room, and instantly "Abe" screamed aloud and flew to him — the ladies, alarmed, thinking it meant fight — and alighted upon his shoulder, pressing his bald head against his cheek with a familiar "How do you do, my old friend of battle times?"

NORTHWEST SANITARY FAIR.

As a civilian, our Eagle has made himself very useful. The patriotic reader will remember how earnest and munificent were the people in ministering to the needs of soldiers in the field, and especially to the sick and wounded. Every possible art was used to procure food, clothing, money, books and everything to make them comfortable. As "Abe" had become famous, he was often on exhibition. In the winter of 1864, a grand movement was projected by influential ladies of the West to have a great Fair in Chicago. The following letter, dictated by Gov. James T. Lewis to his Private Secretary, explains a coöperative work:

"STATE OF WISCONSIN, EXECUTIVE DEPARTMENT,
MADISON, *Jan.* 24, 1865.

"J. O. BARRETT, ESQ. *Sir:* Yours of the 17th is received. The Governor directs me to say, in reply, that he cordially approves of your idea of writing a History of the Eagle of the 8th Wisconsin, and feels confident that, in doing so in the way proposed, you may greatly benefit our suffering soldiers. The Governor has no objection to your taking the Eagle to the Fair of the Northwest Sanitary Commission, to be held in Chicago next spring, as suggested, and will see that your wishes in this respect are carried out at the proper time. Respectfully,

"FRANK H. FIRMIN, *Gov. Pr. Sec'y.*"

The history, referred to by the Governor, consisted of detatched sketches of the Eagle, gleaned from such sources as were then available to the author, and sold at the Fair, by A. L. Sewall, netting, with his pictures, $16,000, appropriated for the benefit of the sick and wounded soldiers. Synoptical facts of it appeared in popular magazines and school books, and subsequently were published in E. B. Quiner's "Military History of Wisconsin" (p. 539), Wm. DeLoss Love's "Wisconsin in the War of the Rebellion" (pp. 519 and 769), Chas. R. Tuttle's "Illustrated History of the State of Wisconsin" (p. 458), Mrs. A. H. Hoge's "Boys in Blue" (p. 431).

The Eagle was taken to the Chicago Fair — opened May 30th, with military ceremonies — under the auspices of the State, together with the flags and other relics and trophies, entrusted to the superintendence of J. H. McFarland, State Armorer, and to John F. Hill, as assistant. His place was in the "Eagle Department," central amid the paraphernalia of war from all parts of the country — amid the vast specimens of agricultural, mineral, commercial and artistic wealth of the nation— amid a world of beauty, intellect and patriotism. Every body went to see this famous bird. Prices for his quills or feathers rose as high as five dollars each, but the demand could seldom be supplied. Not a feather was allowed to be plucked from his beautiful plumage — not for any price. A rich capitalist remarked that he would " give $10,000 for that Eagle ;" and Mr. Wood, of the Chicago Museum, was authorized by P. T. Barnum to give $20,000 ; but, of course, the proposition to Gov. Lewis was only laughed at. Statesmen, poets, editors, warriors, men and women of all professions paid him their compliments, and, among them, Generals Grant and Sherman, who remarked that they had seen "Old Abe" at different times and places while connected with their armies, mentioning specially "Mississippi Rock and Raymond, Miss., where we had a brush with the enemy."

"OLD ABE'S" REPROOF TO GEN. SHERMAN.

While Gen. Sherman was addressing the people, one day, in the main room of the Exposition Building, fired to enthusiasm over the victory of our arms, mentioning the emblems of the nation around him, and among them the Eagle, he precipitately put out his hand to stroke the plumage of our hero, when he wheeled upon his perch with a savage screech at the General, his white feathers ruffled, trying to fight him for such presumption. The vast audience roared with laughter, when the orator blushingly remarked — "Beat this time!" "Old Abe" would have even victor generals understand, that the plumage of the American Eagle is too sacred to be touched with careless hands.

ARTISTIC TRIBUTE TO OUR WAR-BIRD.

Regarding him as a true American specimen, a Chicago sculptor, Mr. Volk, took a bust of "Old Abe," to crown soldiers' monuments. The following, first published in the *Inter-Ocean*, of March 25, is explanatory:

" Chicago, March 23, 1876.

" J. O. Barrett, Esq. — *Dear Sir:* — In June, 1865,, 'Abe' was brought to my studio, and 'posed' on his perch for a model in clay, full size, of his eagleship. Think I took six or eight sittings. I produced from it a model in plaster, with wings partly spread, and arranged to surmount a monumental shaft or column, holding a flag in its beak, the flag drooping down and covering part of the column. Two of these were made in marble for monuments — one ordered by the cadets of West Point for a monument to a deceased comrade, erected at Macomb, in this State; the other for a soldiers' monument — I forget where it was erected. The model was burnt up in the great fire. When at work on the model of 'Old Abe' I had to keep a sharp lookout for his beak and claws. When I applied the callipers to measure him, and would steal up to him in front, rear or flank as silently as possible, when he appeared asleep, instantly his keen eyes would open with a flash; sometimes he would snatch the callipers with his claws from my hands and drop them to the floor. Occasionally he would give me a dig with his sharp claws and take a piece of skin from my hand with his needle-pointed beak. Sometimes with a shrill screech he would try and break away from his fastenings, floundering about with his powerful wings, which would of course raise a dust and knock things about the studio generally, especially during the absence of his keeper. I think he was heartily glad when the sittings terminated, as he did not appear to relish the confinement, nor did he evince a very high regard for spread-eagle art. But he was a splendid old bird, and behaved himself quite as well as some other two-legged sitters who have honored my studio. I may add that his great namesake sat to me for his bust in 1860. Very respectfully yours, Leonard W. Volk."

In the Chicago *Tribune* of June 2, 1865, B. F. Taylor thus word-paints " Old Abe " in the alcove:

" And there, the bird of our banner holds grand levee from day to day, his white crest like the snowy plume of Henry of Navarre, that eye upon you that can look undazzled on the sun. The Eagle of Chippewa — the children have plucked the bird out of the old flag and have set him living at the head of their legions. We bare our brow to him, the grandest contributor to the Fair, and we leave the strangely assorted group to the reader: the tattered, bloody colors yonder, and then the little shoe-maker that has a heart in it, and the Eagle that *ought* to have a soul to be saved — harmonious workers in mercy's sweet rivalry."

MILWAUKEE SOLDIERS' HOME FAIR.

Milwaukee had been a home for the sick and

wounded soldiers; during the year ending Apr. 15, 1865, in one single building on West Water St. were entertained 8,000 soldiers, representing different parts of the country; having a reputation for patriotism and charity, and the object being so noble, to venture was to succeed in building a permanent "Soldiers' Home." Every branch of business in the State and country at large was represented. There in magnificent profusion were our fine arts in conspicuous display, our educational interests, relics of all the wars of the nation and of by-gone times of men and deeds now historic, specimens illustrative of geological and natural history, our State and National literature and patriotism. But a short time prior, Lincoln had been martyred, and anything associated with his memory was of peculiar attraction, even to the "assassination flags"—the one that caught Booth's spur and the one the President seized when shot. As the Wisconsin War-Eagle bore his "Yankee Name," and was renowned for his military exploits, he was, as ever before, the central figure in that vast array of wealth and grandeur. His position was outside the massive main building, on Huron St., in a large tent, entitled "Tangled Feature," superintended by Mr. McCracken, but placed under the special charge of John F. Hill, who brought him from Chicago. In the center of this tent were extensive evergreen rings, rising one above another, and at the topmost was a pretty circular platform whereon the Eagle sat, "monarch of all I survey," for below him were mud-turtles, peacocks, Devon cows, sheep, cranes, hawks, owls, rabbits, foxes, badgers, doves, a bloodhound, a bear, a coon which the 12th Wis.

Battery had in the war, and afterwards gave to the State, and "four other eagles, on their several perches, of different species," said the *Sentinel* of June 30, "called respectively 'Old Abe,' the famous battle Eagle of the 8th Wis., 'Gen. Grant,' 'Phil. Sheridan' and 'Gen. McClellan.'" But "Abe" had the uppermost seat of honor. The *Home Fair Journal* thus describes this hero of twenty-five battles:

"Beneath a canopy of green, sits the Veteran Eagle, 'Old Abe,' the bird that for three long years was the companion of the gallant boys of the Eighth Wisconsin Regiment, marching and camping and going into battle with them; and when the battle grew hot, and threatened death to all, leaving his perch, and soaring aloft with a scream that rose above the roar of battle, he cheered his companions to victory. With an eye that seems as if it would pierce you through, he calmly and with the profoundest dignity, surveys the visitors, as if he were looking down in pity upon them. There is something grand in his presence, and, as you look upon him, you cannot but feel that you are looking upon an important personage; and verily you are, for has he not been in the service of his country? and has he not contributed thousands of dollars to the relief of his companions in arms? Looking upon the splendid bird, we did not wonder that the eagle was chosen by the war-like and all-conquering Romans as their emblem, nor, that he was chosen by the liberty-loving patriots of the Revolution as the emblem of the new Republic."

"OLD ABE'S" PICTURES, AND THEIR PROFITS.

One of the practical methods to raise money at the Milwaukee Soldiers' Home Fair was, by the sale of "Old Abe's" pictures. In the years to come, after he has "gone to glory," these will be of peculiar interest to new generations that read and ponder over our late war of rival civilizations. Appreciating this fact, a gentleman in Rockford, Ill., has carefully preserved a copy and the history of every picture thus far taken of the bird; and has arranged them in a "Pictorial Chart of Old Abe." His description of them is interesting :

"1. 'Childhood picture,' photographed by A. J. Devor, in Eau Claire, summer of 1861, certified to as a correct likeness by Capt. V. Wolf; heraldic and serenely prophetic in look and attitude. 2. The bird wearied from unaccustomed excitement; taken by J. S. Fuller, in Madison, when the regiment was sworn into service, Sept., 1861. 3. The 'Cropped Eagle,' taken by an artist in the South. 4. Lithograph of same for Dunlop, Sewall and Spalding, of Chicago; the original photograph of this 'Soldier picture' is thus referred to by a correspondent of the Milwaukee *Sentinel*, signing himself 'Tompher,' dating his letter at Big Black River, Miss., Oct. 15, 1863: — 'Old Abe, our Eagle, has recently, like everybody else, and because it is a fashion, had his *cart de visite* taken, which, with his biography, will shortly appear in Frank Leslie's Illustrated; his friends will, of course, excuse him if his coat does look a little rough, for he has seen over two years of hard service. The picture includes also the regimental colors with the color guard in position around them; the flags are sadly torn and soiled, and show the marks of the affection of our misguided Southern brethren in every fold.' 5. 'Sanitary picture,' photographed by J. F. Bodtker, in Madison, Apr., 1865; he had 'Old Abe' carried up to the roof of his gallery to obtain a quick light; just as the sun-picture was taking, the free-born Eagle, feeling the inspirations of mountain heights, spread his wings and vaulted into the sky; but the sudden check to the flight by means of his cord, cast perch and bird over the battlement, when, by great presence of mind and superhuman effort, just on the edge of the building, sixty or seventy feet high, the attendant fortunately saved himself and Eagle from a sudden death; carried thence into the gallery rooms, the artist succeeded; about 2,300 of these were sold at the Chicago and Milwaukee Fairs. 6. Lithograph of this was made, same spring, by W. D. Baker, of Chicago, for A. L. Sewall's 'Eagle Army;' used also to illustrate J. O. Barrett's pamphlet sketch of 'Old Abe;' many thousands sold in a few months over all the country and at the Chicago Sanitary Fair, for the benefit of disabled soldiers. 7. Three photographs by E. R. Curtis, in Madison, 1865, representing 'Old Abe' on a cannon captured by the 14th Wis. from the enemy at the battle of Pittsburg Landing, the starry flag for a back ground; about 2,500 of these were sold by Mrs. H. C. Crocker for the Soldiers' Home in Milwaukee. 8. L. Lipman, of Milwaukee, lithographed one of these, and about 8,000 of them were sold by the same lady. 9. Large lithograph for S. W. Martin, giving a synoptical history of the bird. 10. 'Eagle-Bearer picture,' photographed by J. Carbutt, while John F. Hill had his bird at the great Sanitary Fair in Chicago; standing on his war-perch with Mr. Hill patronly guarding 'Old Abe.' 11. In August, 1875, the Wisconsin View Company, of Portage, photographed one, representing the bird on a cannon with perch and flags. 12. 'Centennial photographs,' taken by J. M. Fowler, in Madison, Feb. 7, 1876, representing 'Old Abe' standing with dignity upon his beautiful 'Centennial Perch'—lately constructed; are sharp and well executed; the Governor of Wisconsin, H. Ludington, certifies that 'this picture is a correct likeness of 'Old Abe,' the live War-Eagle.'"

THE OLDEN LEGEND VERIFIED.

The Eagle's feathers and quills — "precious as locks of hair"—have been in as great demand as his pictures. People from England, Scotland and France, many Confederate soldiers and ladies of the South, and patriots in all parts of the Union, having them, seem to think the olden legend is true, that "they condem all other quills which lie near them." Here is a clipping from a private letter of a soldier to his sister, signing himself "A.

T.," dating it "Hamburg, four miles above Pittsburg Landing, Tenn., April 16, 1863." After mentioning several relics of the war for preservation, he says:

"In my miniature case you will find some Confederate scrip; there is also a quill from our Eagle, which Capt. Perkins gave me last evening; the Eagle is flourishing finely."

During the Milwaukee Fair, some reserved feathers and quills of the Eagle were presented to a few personages of note. The Superintendent of "Tangled Feature," having a quill from his wing, presented it to Mrs. G. P. Hewitt, then President of the "Home," with the happy remark, "You are deserving of this." This lady cherishes it as very precious, as it ever recalls those days of sacrifice, and like a magic wand "opens the wounds we seem reluctant to heal." Another was officially presented by the ladies to Gen. B. F. Butler, (subsequently a trustee of the "Home" after its transfer to the United States) with this pleasantry of address, "as it is from the wing of the Wisconsin War-Eagle, it will remind you of our esteem for your patriotic services in a perilous hour of our nation." If there be a reckoning-day for this life's stewardship in the world to come, "Old Abe"—for he has a soul—will be largely credited on sales of pictures, biographies, feathers and tickets of admission to his kingly presence, in that net gain of of $105,000 at this Fair, given to the "Branch Home of the National Asylum for Volunteer Soldiers, established at Milwaukee," munificently endowed by the United States Government, and by Wisconsin to the amount of $5,000.

DEFENDING HIS FEATHERS.

In certain moods "Abe" would even fight the man who presumed to carry off one of his feathers. W. W. Barrett thus describes an experience in Madison, during one of his visits to the bird:

"In company with Geo. W. Baker, then the Eagle's attendant (1875), I called to see 'Old Abe.' He was engaged in eating his breakfast, which consisted of a rabbit fresh from the woods. When we made our appearance, the considerate bird suspended operations and gave his attention to Mr. Baker's salutation of 'Good Morning, Abe,' which he answered with a peculiar shrill voice. Presently my attention was drawn to a white downy feather falling from the body of the Eagle, about six feet distant. Wishing to preserve it for my cabinet of curiosities, I proceeded to pick it up ; but 'Old Abe' was ready to protect his own property, even to the least feather, and, with flashing eyes and angry look, he instantly flew at me with perfect fury, striking hard with his strong, powerful wings, making an effort to disentangle his claws from their fastenings in the rabbit, whose weight, fortunately for me, brought the Eagle to the floor, and I escaped the dangerous charge. Then the enfuriated fellow mounted a tall saw-horse, and there with fierce grips he jumped and leaped about, bristling up his feathers, throwing out his wings, and expressing his anger by frequent and loud screechings. Thus he continued for sometime, indicating he was ready for battle with any foe. We stood at a respectful distance, 'for,' Mr. Baker said, 'his grips are painful and hard to remove when he has taken hold of the flesh." Finally, at the suggestion of Mr. Baker, I seized a broom near at hand, when his attendant ordered him into his own room, but he was defiant and screamed, determined to disobey. Seeing me armed, and Mr. Baker resolute, he reluctantly walked into his own apartment, mounted his perch, and was locked in a 'prisoner of war.'"

But "Old Abe" is generous when his mood inspires it.

Mr. and Mrs. J. O. Culver, of Madison, relate an incident of their innocent little boys that is peculiarly beautiful. Willie and Paul, then eight and four years old, were one day, in the summer of 1869, looking at the bird while in the Capitol Park, when Paul picked up a feather of his lying on the ground, and Willie, noticing its shining luster, exclaimed, "I wish 'Old Abe' would give me a feather." Curious as it may seem, the intelligent bird — whether by accident or design, let the reader say — instantly pulled out a feather from his breast with his beak, and away it sped, waving and dancing on the wind, intently watched by the boys, who at last secured it as it fell on the other side of the Park.

SOLDIERS AND SAILORS' CONVENTION AT PITTSBURG.

Our famous bird has also been " round the circle," on great occasions of public interest relating to the government, especially at military reviews and conventions. It will be recollected, that immediately following the surrender of the Confederate army in 1865, new and intricate perils menaced the country on every hand, most difficult to adjust to the satisfaction of North and South. Indeed it was the darkest hour of the Rebellion; for President Andy Johnson and Congress were antagonistic as to measures of reconstruction. Under these national troubles, a mass gathering of the patriotic people, entitled the " Soldiers and Sailors' Convention," was called to meet in the city of Pittsburg, Pa., on the 25th and 26th of September, 1866, with a view to " sustain the measures adopted by Congress for the restoration of the Union." It was one of the most magnificent outbursts of popular feeling ever manifested in the history of our country, and combined the most versatile array of talent and military prestige. There were representatives from all the Northern States and some of the Southern — the Great West preponderating in numbers — and among them were Gens. Cox, Willich, Schenck, Leggett and Garfield, of Ohio; Gens. Butler and Banks, of Mass.; Gens. Allen and Bintliff, Cols. Bartlett, Butterick and Goodwin, and Capt. Langworthy, of Wis.; Col. A. D. Straight, of Indiana, of Andersonville Prison renown; Gens. Gerry and Negley, and Gov. Curtin, of Pa.; Gen. Sigel, of Maryland; Gen. Sprague, of R. I.; Gen. Farnsworth, of Ill.; Gens. Cochrane, Barnum, Barlow, Hawkins, Gregg and Martindale, of New York; Gens. Terry and Hawley, of Conn.; Gens. Baxter and Allen, of Mich.; and, sitting side by side with them on the platform, to indicate the democratic spirit of the convention, were such privates as L. Edwin Dudley, "the patriotic clerk of Washington;" Robert Hendershott, "the Drummer Boy of the Rappahannock;" John Burns, "the heroic volunteer of Gettysburg, who fought in defense of his own home," and Serg. Geo. Robinson, of Maine, who saved the life of Secretary Seward on the night of the assassination of President Lincoln.

It was also fitting that our War-Eagle should represent Wisconsin at that convention. Under the escort of his favorite friend, Capt. McDonald, he had a constant ovation on the way thither, arriving at his destination on the eve of the 24th. In that crowded city,

the celebrated Eagle had safe quarters in a parlor of the
St. Charles Hotel, with sixty or more "other soldiers of
the war," paying extra, of course, for the special honor
of such a room.   The city was gorgeous, the excitement
intense, the feeling resolute to defend the attitude of
Congress.   The City Hall, in which the convention was
held, was decorated with evergreens, flowers and flags;
between the windows hung badges of twenty-five army
corps, and on the platform were the emblems of war
and of peace, in the form of white flags and sheaves of
wheat.   Over the door of entrance was this motto —
"*There can be no lasting peace while the flag of the Union
cannot wave unmolested over the graves of our fallen comrades.*"

The hall was densely packed; in one of the aisles
stood delegates from a neighborhood sixty strong,
every one of whom had been wounded in the service,
and had their colors riddled.   The jam of people was
so great at the door, Capt. McDonald found it impossible to advance with his Eagle; but just as Gen. B. F.
Butler commenced speaking on his own resolution, at
this first session of the convention, the chairman, Gen.
J. D. Cox, interrupting, requested him to pause a moment, shouting with a loud voice — "Here comes 'Old
Abe,' the veteran War-Eagle of Wisconsin; please open
the way, gentlemen, that he may come forward."   The
crowd defiled right and left, and as the captain walked
up the aisle with that monarch bird so majestic on his
perch, the vast audience spontaneously rose and cheered
him — once, twice, thrice — with a ring that jarred the
very roof, when the Eagle flapped his wings and screamed

aloud his war-cry of battle. On motion of Gen. Ham lin, of Maine, "Old Abe," was assigned a position of honor on the platform. The Wisconsin *State Journal* of September 27, speaks of the incident, by a reporter:

" The moment quiet had been restored, an event occurred that seemed to set all wild. The 'Old Abe' Eagle which the 8th Wisconsin carried through its service, was brought up the aisle, perched on the top of a staff; the body rose and cheered him; the band played, and the kingly bird flapped his wings lustily as if he recognized the old music, the old cheers, and the old flags. 'Abe' was then seated near the chairman on his perch amid the emblems of peace, fully alive to the scene, responding to nearly all the cheers, as Gen. Butler harangued the people, by flapping his wings."

TORCH-LIGHT PROCESSION.

That evening of the 25th was improved by a torch-light procession of five miles long, Gen. Negley chief marshal, fifteen thousand persons moving in it, the sol-diers carrying torch-lights, others insignia of war and peace." "The streets," said the Wisconsin *Journal* of the 27th, " were ablaze and filled for miles with people. Such popular enthusiasm has seldom been equalled. The city was one glorious illumination of blazing banners and sentiments steeped in fire. There was an unsurpassed display of beautiful designs, and models in brilliant lights in moving lines." First came the " Boys in Blue," next the Fire Department, next the Undine Boat Club, with the motto, " We will pull together," and then " the Wisconsin War-Eagle," with his Bearer and other dignitaries, seated on his perch encircled with ribbons of red, white and blue, in an open carriage drawn by four white horses; as he passed along through the thronged avenues of Pittsburg, there was a continuous tempest of cheers and shouts, and exclamations — " Here he comes! " when showers of flowers would be thrown into his carriage literally loading it down, while he, unspoiled by such adulations, kept his grave dignity like a white-headed sire of the Revolution, amid a profusion of patriotic mottoes, and the *devoirs* of the enraptured multitude.

SOLDIERS' MONUMENT, PEORIA, ILL.

It was dedicated October 11, 1866. Thirty to forty thousand persons were present, largely represented by veterans of the war. The Peoria *Daily Transcript,* of October 12, says:

" The dedication of the Soldiers' Monument, yesterday, drew together by far the largest crowd that Peoria ever saw within her limits. The day was beautiful; a soft haze overspread the sky, and a mellow tint of summer veiled the sun, putting the atmosphere in that peculiar condition in which the greatest sound is transmitted. * * In the forenoon, the streets about the Court House Square began to fill, and before long the Peoria House was surrounded by an excited throng hurrahing for Butler and Logan. "Old Abe," the veteran Eagle of the 8th Wisconsin regiment, was brought out to the balcony, and was greeted by the audience and many of his old companions in arms with vociferous cheers. The noble bird was under the care of Capt. A. R. McDonald. State Armorer of Wisconsin, and Capt. A. G. Weissert, of the 8th Wisconsin Volunteers."

The procession, with "Old Abe" for high honors, was most imposing. The monument, with names of the heroic dead thus perpetuated, was covered with evergreens, wreaths and flowers up the white shaft and over the eagle crowning its top. "Old Abe" was carried to the speakers' stand within those now sacred grounds, where he was greeted by long continued cheering. The speeches of Generals B. F. Butler, John A. Logan and R. G. Ingersoll, were the more electrifying for the presence of the veteran Eagle, that reminded them of times now historic, as described by Henry Howard Brownell, Lieut. U. S. Navy, in his "War-Lyrics," wherein he rapturously pictures the magnificence of "The Eagle at Corinth":

"'Tis many a stormy day
    Since, out of the cold, bleak North,
    Our great War-Eagle sailed forth
To swoop o'er battle and fray.
Many and many a day
    O'er charge and storm hath he wheeled,
    Foray and foughten field,
        Tramp, and volley and rattle!—
    Over crimson trench and turf,
    Over climbing clouds of surf,
Through tempest and cannon-rack,
    Have his terrible pinions whirled—
        (A thousand fields of battle!
        A million leagues of foam!)
But our Bird shall yet come back,
    He shall soar to his Eyrie-Home—
    And his thunderous wing be furled,
    In the gaze of a gladdened world,
        On the Nation's loftiest Dome!"

BUILDING AN ORPHANS' HOME.

Through the long and praiseworthy efforts of Mrs. C. A. P. Harvey, wife of the lamented Governor who was drowned while on a mission of mercy, a Soldiers' Or-

phans' Home was established at Madison, designed for
the orphans of fallen soldiers; and "Old Abe," of
course, as in other benevolent enterprises, must help
build it. At the State Fair, held in Janesville, Sept.
25, 1865, a tent was erected in which "Old Abe," borne
by Wm. J. Jones, was exhibited under the management
of Mrs. Harvey, earning, with other aids, $427. Up to
this date, this "Eagle-Benefactor" had gained about
$25,000 for soldiers and their orphans.

SOLDIERS AND SAILORS' CONVENTION AT CHICAGO.

On the 19th of May, 1868, a "Soldiers and Sailors'
Convention" was held in Chicago, represented by all
the States of the North and some of the South, Gen.
Lucius Fairchild, of Wisconsin, chairman; followed
the next day by the National Republican Convention,
with Carl Schurz for chairman, which nominated U. S.
Grant for President of the United States. The *Wisconsin State Journal,* of May 20, says:

"The Soldiers and Sailors' Convention was largely attended.
Formed procession at 11 A. M., and marched to Turner Hall.
The procession was headed by the Wisconsin delegation, who
carried 'Old Abe,' the War-Eagle, in the van. The flags of the
Wisconsin delegation were borne to the front by Gen. J. M. Rusk
and Hon. M. H. Sessions. The procession was three-quarters of
a mile in length and four soldiers deep. The streets along the
entire route were thronged with people. The march was full
of life and incident; the line joining in singing their old battle-
songs as in the Southern marches. Upon entering the hall, the
scene was one of wildest enthusiasm, cheer on cheer being given
for the portrait of Grant which hung over the platform, the bust
of Lincoln which stood upon the rostrum, and for 'Old Abe,'
the War-Eagle, who was fastened upon his perch in front of the
platform."

A reporter of a Chicago paper, speaking of the same convention, says :

* * "And when the resolution proposing Gen. U. S. Grant as candidate for the Presidency was passed, as the vast multitude rose and cheered, and the band struck up 'Hail to the Chief,' 'Old Abe,' as if understanding it all, stretched high his proud form and repeatedly flapped his wings in approbation of the nomination."

SOLDIERS' REUNIONS.

"Old Abe's" presence at all western military gatherings is as essential as the old flag. The soldiers of Wisconsin met in Milwaukee, Sept. 27th and 28th, 1870, Gov. Fairchild presiding over the convention, liberally represented by "veterans who bore the battle flags they fought under, many of them torn into shreds by the storms of lead through which they had passed, but esteemed more highly on that account."

"Gen. H. E. Paine" [in whose valiant army "Old Abe" at one time served], says the Milwaukee *Sentinel* of the 26th, "was introduced, and, in very eloquent words, welcomed his old comrades, all soldiers of Wisconsin and other States, who fought so nobly in the late war against rebellion. Gov. Fairchild was called for, and spoke a cordial word to his old comrades. Gen. Hobart then addressed the meeting; but before doing so, he introduced one of the most distinguished personages of the late war — 'Old Abe.' The Eagle was then brought out, amid great applause."

A poem was read by Col. Chas. H. Clark, one verse of which, alluding to "Abe," is as follows:

"Our Eagle's high behest
To crown our banner's crest —
Our standard true —

> Unfurl it to the breeze
> From mast head on seas —
> Guard of our liberties —
> Red, white and blue."

"At the close of this reading," says the Milwaukee *Sentinel* of the 28th, "'Old Abe,' the War-Eagle, was brought upon the stage by Capt. McDonald, and was received with rapturous applause." One of the grandest military demonstrations ever known in the State, was given the next day on the fair grounds; address by Hon. Matt. H. Carpenter. The Eagle, acting his part of heraldry, was there, the admired of thirty thousand people.

At a subsequent Reunion in Milwaukee (1875), after hours of military parade through the streets, in a cold rain, the feathers almost freezing, "Abe" got chilled and had to abandon the post of honor. Immediately carried home to Madison, he was soon restored to health. In the spring prior to this event, he was so sick he could not stand up, but rolled over and drooped, as if about to enter the paradise in store for all patriotic eagles. Hugh Lewis, his attendant, took him into the office of the Superintendent of Public Property, blanketed him, poured medicated water down his throat, nursed him with devoted vigilance, and, in three days, he was on his perch again as good as new. The longevity of an eagle is remarkable, sometimes living, it is said, a hundred years. If "Abe" could be more free in his selection of food and toughened to storms and tempests, he might live when empires rise and fall. Warring against the enemies of his country is his best regimen of health. Wilson, the Ornithologist, speaking of the longevity of an eagle, draws this happy moral:

"It has not, like men, invented rich wines, ardent spirits and a thousand artificial poisons, in the form of soups, sauces and sweetmeats. Its food is simple, indulges freely, uses great exercise, breathes the purest air, is healthy, vigorous and long lived. The lords of creation themselves might derive some useful hints from these facts, were they not already, in general, too wise, or too proud, to learn from their *inferiors*, the fowls of the air and the beasts of the field."

Again, to keep alive the spirit of '61, "Old Abe," borne by Capt. McDonald, was carried to Soldiers' Reunions in such Wisconsin cities as Fond du Lac, Burlington, Elkhorn, Evansville and La Crosse. The Army of the Tennessee — "Old Abe" fought in that, when that now consecrated river was made the "Pass of Thermopylæ." Its sixth annual Reunion was held in Madison, July 3d and 4th, 1870. Among the notabilities of the 20,000 people there gathered, were Generals Pope, Sheridan, Atwood, Washburn, Slack, of Indiana, Noyes, of Ohio, and Gen. "Old Abe," of Wisconsin, with

"The colors, ragg'd in a hundred fights,
And the dusty Frocks of Blue."

At a Reunion of company K, in Racine, August 31, 1871, he greeted his old "soldier boys" again, with a special recognition to Col. James O. Bartlett, who led the gallant Eighth in some of its hardest battles. He was in Neillsville, Oct. 9, 1871, where were represented fifty-two military organizations, himself the personation of valorous dignity, "as the American bird ought to be on such occasions," says the Clark County *Republican,*

8

"watched with the greatest interest and curiosity by the immense crowd." "Old Abe" was also an invited guest at a Reunion of the valiant 1st Wisconsin, in Madison, February 22, 1872, Gen. Starkweather at the head as in the conflict of arms. He was perched in the arched doorway between the rooms (in Park Hotel), keeping a grave silence during the reading of Hon. A. M. Thomson's felicitous poem and speech of Gen. Fairchild. But while Hon. James Ross was making a ringing response to the toast, "The Federal Union — may wisdom cement what valor saved," he joined in the patriotic sentiment vociferously. The words of L. J. Bates, in the song entitled "'Old Abe,' the Battle Eagle," music by T. Martin Towne, seemed to sing of themselves at such gatherings, in remembrance of the fallen and the surviving of the victor soldiers:

> "They come, but the ranks are shrunken and thin;
> Oh! large be the welcome that gathers them in!
> They come with the flags in the glad sunlight,
> A cloud of peace, that is feathery white;
> And still o'er the standards they bear on high,
> There hovers the Eagle of Victory —
> Hurrah for the Eagle, our bold battle-Eagle!
> The terror of traitors and king of the sky!"

GRAND ARMY OF THE REPUBLIC.

Since the war, one of the most enthusiastic demonstrations of popular patriotism ever known in our country, occurred in Chicago, at the "Reunion of the Grand Army of the Republic," commencing on May 12th and ending May 14, 1875. It was represented by such personages as Gov. Hartranft, of Pennsylvania, Gov. Pinchback, of Louisiana, Gen. Phil. Sheridan, Gen. W. T. Sherman, Gov. Beveridge, of Illinois, Gen. Harlow, Secretary of State, Hon. Thos. S. Ridgeway, State Treasurer, of Illinois; and, of the Wisconsin delegation, were Capt. F. W. Oakley, U. S. Marshal, and Cols. Thomas Reynolds and B. Hancock; gentlemen and ladies of all professions were there, indicating the deep gratitude the people cherish toward the deliverers of our country from the thraldom of oppressive law and institution.

The Grand Pacific Hotel was the headquarters of the "Army of the Republic," "Old Abe," borne by Hugh Lewis, occupying the office with the rest. H. M. Page, reporting for the Madison *State Journal,* of May 14th, says:

"Nothing evoked so much enthusiasm as Wisconsin's bird of freedom. He has been the center of attraction at the Pacific Hotel, where his perch was flanked by the United States and State flags, and where veterans from different parts of the country, from Wisconsin, Iowa, Minnesota, Illinois, Michigan, Indiana, Missouri, West Virginia, and we know not how many more States, who had known the bird in the army, rallied around him and recalled the many fields on which they had seen him with the Eighth Wisconsin."

On the 13th, a procession was formed, and it was estimated 150,000 people were packed together along the line of march, to say nothing of the large numbers who witnessed it from the windows. The Chicago *Times,* of May 14th, thus describes this pageantry of arms:

"The fifth division rested on West Washington street. In this part of the line marched the Grand Army Posts, Gen. H. Hilliard, the State Commander of the Order, heading the procession, as marshal, with a staff of ten. The Great Western Light Guard

Band furnished the music. The Sterling City Guards, com
manded by Capt. J. W. R. Stanbough, preceded the several Posts
of the Grand Army. They were followed by a carriage, containing 'Old Abe,' the Veteran War-Eagle of the Eighth Wisconsin, and his escort consisting of Capt. F. W. Oakley, U. S.
Marshal, Dr. A. J. Ward and Hugh Lewis, of the Iron Brigade,
Capt. A. R. McDonald and Ex-Mayor Leitch, of Madison, Wis.
'Abe' was perched upon a shield, held aloft by one of his
guards of honor, and he was loudly cheered wherever the
crowd caught sight of him. He frequently flapped his wings
and looked majestic."

The Chicago *Tribune,* of the 14th, mentioning the
" grizzly rain " that fell in the afternoon of the second
day's proceedings, says:

"The greatest feature of the procession, aside from the Veteran organization, composed of men who know what it is to be a
soldier, and whose tattered regimental flags indicated the services they had done, was the War-Eagle, 'Old Abe,' a noted
leader of the Eighth Wisconsin; he was the chief lion of the
day, sitting upon his perch with immense dignity, flapping his
wings and screaming like a mortal bird of freedom on the now
obsolete twenty-dollar gold piece."

As the procession approached the Exposition Building, where the reception was to be given Gov. Beveridge
by a presentation of national colors, the enthusiasm was
intensified; old veterans, seeing the War Eagle in his
splended barouche with his escort, threw their hats into
it and high into the air, loudly cheering, others loading
it with flowers, while several ladies, flying to the carriage, presented the Bearer a large wreath of beautiful
roses set in evergreens, in the form of a massive hoop
which was immediately put around the perch, the Eagle
sitting within it, scanning the balcony on which were

assembled the civil and military officers, surrounded by flags and festoons that covered the pillars and hung in graceful folds from the cornices; and, as the vast multitude cheered and cheered, " Old Abe " responded by his majestic art of speech, as if really conscious of personating the liberty for which he and his comrades fought.

TABLEAU OF "OLD ABE."

The idea was unique. Under the leadership of Mrs. J. G. Thorp, President of the " Women's State Centennial Executive," a representative meeting of the Centennial Clubs of the State was called to the capital to rekindle the fires of patriotism by a historic celebration of Independence Day, on the evening of July 5, 1875. Her daughter, Mrs. Ole Bull, wife of the celebrated musician, was the art designer of this *beau ideal* in exhibition. "It was an ovation," says the State *Journal*, " of which we might be proud to speak. The Speaker's desk in the Assembly Room of the Capitol had been transformed by artistic hands into a niche with the State Insignia, before which hung a mysterious curtain. On the opposite side of the hall, a mossy grotto, enshrining the flower nymphs, added its own charms to the scene."

" The Day we Celebrate," the personation of King George's time by Gen. Geo. B. Smith, the floral exuberance, the elegant addresses of Hon. E. G. Ryan, and Col. W. B. Slaughter, the representative Gen. Washington, making his " first visit to the fair young widow, Mrs. Custis, who with her two children playing at her feet is surprised at his entrance," the proffer of the services of

Gen. LaFayette to Washington to help fight the battles of American liberty, were indeed a life-drama of the Revolution, seldom surpassed in beauty of personation; but another scene eclipsed it all. When the curtain rose, there stood the famous War-Eagle on his perch, surrounded by State and National flags and stands of arms, as the living ideal of our prowess a hundred years ago. Maj. C. G. Mayers, in costume of Paul Jones, which renewed his youth, recited in a very spirited manner the following poem, by Lizzie Doten, entitled:

THE EAGLE OF FREEDOM.

" O, land of our glory, our boast and our pride.
  Where the brave and the fearless for freedom have died.
  How clear is the lustre that beams from thy name!
  How bright on thy brow are the laurels of fame!
  The stars of thy Union still burn in the sky,
  And the scream of thine Eagle is heard from on high!
  His eyrie is built where no foe can invade,
  Nor traitors prevail with the brand and the blade!

Ch. — The Eagle of Freedom, in danger and night,
    Keeps watch o'er our flag from his star-circled heigh,
    From mountain and valley, from hill-top and sea,
    Three cheers for the Eagle, the Bird of the Free!
        Hurrah! Hurrah!
    Hurrah for the Eagle, the Bird of the Free!

Mount up, O thou Eagle! and rend in thy flight
The war-cloud that hides our broad banner from sight!
Guard, guard it from danger, though war-rent and worn,
And see that no star from its azure is torn!
Keep thy breast to the storm, and thine eye on the sun,
Till, true to our motto, THE MANY ARE ONE!
Till the red rage of war with its tumult shall cease,
And the dove shall return with the olive of peace.
                           — CHORUS.

O, sons of the mighty, the true and the brave,
The souls of your heroes rest not in their grave;
The holy libation to Liberty poured,
Hath streamed, not in vain, from the blood-crimsoned sword.
Henceforth with your Star Spangled Banner unfurled,
Your might shall be felt to the ends of the world,
And rising Republics, like nebulæ gleam,
Wherever the stars of your nation shall beam.

Ch.—The Eagle of Freedom, sublime in his flight,
Shall rest on your banner, encircled with light;
And then shall the chorus, in unison be,
Three cheers for the Eagle, the Bird of the Free!
Hurrah! Hurrah!
Hurrah for the Eagle, the Bird of the Free!"

"Old Abe" modestly listened to the recital of this poem, as if conscious of the scrutiny of that refined audience. This uncommon mood of the bird is thus described by two lady Secretaries of the Centennial, Mrs. J. D. Butler and Mrs. B. W. Jones, in their authorized report of the Exhibition, as given in the *State Journal* of July 7:

"Our grand 'Old Abe,' the winged veteran of many a battle field, mounted on his perch, stood in the most dignified manner during Col. C. G. Mayers' poetical address; and, though he could gaze at the sun and brave the roar of the cannon, he drooped his head as if scarcely worthy of the Colonel's eulogy."

"OLD ABE" IN A DANCE!

Why not? He is a United States citizen, and so entitled to all its social amenities. Under the auspices of the "Women's Centennial," "Mr. Eagle," of the Eighth Wisconsin, received a card of invitation to attend a "Legislative Leap Year Party," in the Assembly Cham-

bers, on the eve of February 17, 1876. The Terpsi-
chorean drama opened with the Marseillaise Hymn, by
Mrs. H. M. Page, who, attired in appropriate costume,
appeared as the "Daughter of the Regiment," admirably singing and tapping her drum, with accompani-
ments from Bach's Band. The war-bird, on his "Centennial Perch," stood one side, a little in front of the
vivandiere, listening with a noticeable dignity, animated
most at the sound of the drum that recalled the *reveille*
of other days, and when she closed singing the "Star
Spangled Banner," feeling the deep inspiration of the
audience, he encored with clapping of wings. Not being specially trained to dance, he was excused further
military attentions, and retired to the "Eagle Department."

MEDALLION OF "OLD ABE."

History, song, art — the legacy of our laureate Eagle.
The last crowning excellence is a *medallion* for the
Women's Department of the Wisconsin Centennial, the
voluntary contribution of Mrs. Culver, of Madison.
The following letter from the gifted artist, is explana-
tory of the beautiful design:

"MADISON, March 23, 1876.

"J. O. BARRETT, Esq. *Dear Sir:* — In answer to your inquiries concerning the portrait of the 8th Wis. Eagle, which is
to be painted for the Centennial Exposition, I would say that it
is to be something less than half life-size, on a gilt medallion,
to be framed in carved ebony and placed upon the top of an
ebony cabinet. This State Cabinet is to contain the books and
music written by the women of Wisconsin, also choice orna-
ments and specimens of art. The panels in the sides and doors

of the lower part are to be decorated with flowers, grasses and vines, done in oil. The upper part is open, the shelves are irregular, after the Japanese style, and are surrounded by elegant hand-carving, executed by Mr. G. Haug, of Milwaukee. On Wednesday, the 15th of March, 'Old Abe' honored me with a sitting; he was attended by his keeper, to whom he seems greatly attached. I was astonished at the color and expression of his eye, which forcibly reminded me of the description given by a countryman, who said: 'The Eagle has a *shrill* eye!' and at the size and cruel strength of his beak, which had the appearance of yellow ivory. The sharp look of inquiry he gave me seemed to ask, 'what is all this bother about, anyway?' Fortunately, for my peace of mind, the mahl-stick seemed to make this king of birds quail. He stood upon his standard with the the United States shield beneath him, gazing over the waters of Mendota with a far-off look, but a tap of my brush on the easel would recall his thoughts, and cause him to turn his head quickly in the desired position. It was in one of these moments of surprise, that I caught the expression of his 'shrill' eye. When nearly through with the sitting, the flag was draped in his talons over the standard; the sight of the 'stars and stripes' seemed to arouse old memories, and he uttered several screams which I thought might mean a declaration of war. His keeper assured me, however, that it was only a feeling of joy that animated him; but as he began to tear the bunting with his great beak in a very decided manner, and as his meal time was approaching, he having fasted two or three days as is his custom, this part of the picture was rapidly executed, and he went off to his dinner of rabbit, which I hope he enjoyed as fully as I did my morning with 'Old Abe.'

"Very Respectfully,

"MINNIE B. CULVER."

ADVENTURE OF AN EAGLE BEARER.

Among the "Chippewa Eagle Boys" is John F. Hill, brother of Thomas, both of Company C; their father was killed in the battle of Petersburg. John enlisted when he was sixteen. In the battle of Corinth, Hill was standing beside the Eagle, near Mc-Lane; had fired six times, and was just putting on a cap for another discharge, when a Minie ball struck his right arm at the joint of the elbow and glanced off into his side, passing clear through him. He fell instantly. Seeing this favorite boy lying there, a soldier ran to Capt. Wolt declaring, "Johny Hill is killed!" "Never mind," replied the Captain, "we cannot attend to dead men now." Soon after this, the Captain himself passed the spot, looked at him, rolled him over, and pronounced him dead; then with his sword he hacked the bark of a tree near by, that he might be more readily found after the battle. Our army fell back; the rebels advanced, passing our wounded soldier. Four hours he lay there weltering in his blood, the pulse of life feebly beating. Coming to his consciousness about dark, he rose to his feet, and, with a staggering gait started for the Union camp, but had not gone far when he was taken prisoner, and turned back, fainting at intervals on the way. By midnight he had walked four miles to the rebel hospital, where he was obliged to lie out all that rainy night under a tree. Some time during the darkness, after the rebel wounded were cared for, John respectfully entreated the Surgeon to dress his wound.

"Dress *your* wound?" replied the "Southern gentlemen," "what's the use? You wont live till morning!"

O, the painful hours — how slowly they dragged the night! Three o'clock — four o'clock — six o'clock — morning! and yet he lives, unpitied, untouched, save by the sweet heavens that wept over him. In due time the Surgeon went the rounds among his patients, inquiring after their condition, and finding John steaming in the wet, shouted: "Hello, Yank, you are alive yet, ar'n't ye?"

"Guess I am," faintly answered the resolute boy.

"Well, you'll fag out to-day — it's going to be —— hot! Eat that if you want," said the good hearted Surgeon, throwing him some parched corn.

About 12 M., the rebels began to retreat, when a cavalry man rushed into the hospital, saying: "All that are able to walk, come with me—the Yanks are driving us!"

Just as the word was spoken, and a portion had left, John staggered to the same Surgeon, and asked him if he had any objection to his going to Corinth.

"No!—you can't go a rod from where you are standing," answered the rebel, with an oath.

John now began his snail-like journey to his friends, the blood from his side frothing out at every motion. That morning Thomas (the brother) procured a spade and picaxe, and a headboard on which he had recorded the sad epitaph, and, thus equipped, hurried to find the tree marked by Capt. Wolf, there expecting to bury the body of his dead brother. Thus the two boys were approaching each other, but by different routes, not far apart, however. At a distance, John saw Thomas, and spoke as loud as he could—"Thomas!"

Thus interrogated, Thomas looked here and there, and at last discerned a straggler, but did not at first recognize him. Again John called, "Thomas, it's *me!*"

Thomas approached, and, when within a few rods, recognized his brother, and chokingly articulated: " *You,*—John? *John!*"

Imagine the happy meeting—the dead alive again! John leaned upon his brother's arm, and thus was helped into Corinth, where he was tenderly cared for by our Surgeon. When his wound was dressed, he fainted, but soon revived. That night the Surgeon gave orders to watch John, stating he would probably die before morning. It is hard to kill a soldier. He recovered, and is now able to do light work as a worthy citizen. He remained in the service another year, at one time faithfully fulfilling the duties of the Adjutant's Orderly. As already mentioned, John handsomely bore "Old Abe," for a while during "the soldier time," and at the great Sanitary Fairs of Chicago and Milwaukee, in 1865. By appointment of Gov. Ludington he now has the honor of bearing the proud bird to the Centennial, as

"A type of the sons of Liberty."

1876!

The Centennial of America, the test of democratic government for a hundred years; what a convocation of peoples from all the earth; what a reminiscence of valor; what a pledge of National faith! The war is over; brothers that fought each other meet again, hand to hand, unarmed, heart in the hand, and a grand cheer for freedom. Our tears commingle over the graves of the " Blue and the Gray;" our spears cross there in solemn oath to defend the old "stars and stripes;" we swear before the God of our Fathers, presiding over the destinies of America — that no enemy, within or without, shall sever the " Union of States."

" Honest Old Abe " fell with the last gasp of the Rebellion; his enemies, even, bowed their heads in grief over the martyr; the generous of their brave natures was too great to repress, when he rose like a Christ amid the glory of an emancipated race; but the Eagle of the country for which men fought and died, the historic " Old Abe," still lives as the seal of good-will between rivals in the tournament of war, and may live till a new century dawns in a brighter age. His head is a beautiful *white;* it is peace in emblem — the pure of justice wreathing the sun-lighted eyes of liberty, that speak so much of battle and honor. This " Bird of Lincoln " has seen the ending of the dreadful war in which he was engaged, the North and South united again in closer bonds than ever — brothers now — the National Constitution reconstructed to protect each race and sex, and the resurrection of this Republic to a higher civilization that preludes a Continental Union, by and by, bounded only by oceans, under one common flag.

The Wisconsin Legislature of 1876, by joint resolution of the Assembly and Senate, authorized Gov. H. Ludington to have "Old Abe" borne by some veteran soldier, on exhibition at Philadelphia, where first such a bird was placed in our Constellation of States; where he is to demonstrate by his military *personnel* how happily chosen was the emblem, and how much the "War-Eagle of Wisconsin," that never lost a battle, is a "Declaration of Independence," by the grandeur of his mien and the keenness of his justice.

To the royal visitors who may there gaze upon this famous bird, he teaches, by the unquenchable fire of his patriotism, the lessons of ages to them as to ourselves, that injustice even to one human being is so much governmental fealty lost, that compromise with oppression breeds the giant of rebellion, that war comes as a painful necessity when we neglect to protect the inalienable rights of man; and, while the superior strength and durability of a republican form of government in maintaining itself against external and internal enemies, and thence the evolution of the greatest possible progress in wealth, intelligence, individual sovereignty and domestic virtue, is unmistakably demonstrated to the nations of the earth for a hundred years — that, to ensure such progress for the future, nationalty needs to be nurtured simply as a component of universal brotherhood; then will our Eagle be no longer fettered to the march of armies, but free in his native

skies — the hovering cherubim of a cosmopolitan citizenship, of a Representative Congress of Nations in
prudent council to settle all local difficulties without
the arbitrament of the sword — free in commerce, international in science, eclectic in religion.

> " And then we'll raise, on Liberty's broad base,
> A structure of wise government, and show,
> In our new world, a glorious spectacle
> By reason swayed, self-governed, self-improved,
> And the electric chain of public good
> Twined round the public happiness of each;
> And every heart thrilled by the pariot chord
> That sounds the glory of America."

"UNDER ARMS, ONCE MORE!"

[There is a grandeur in the death of Patriots, when it opens a Nation to
the life and light of our Fatherland in the Heavens. Where is our Lincoln?
Where, the heroes that went down with him, pale, brave, trustful, to the
brink of the river, and crossed it under convoy of fleets manned by the im-
mortals of the "Ancient of Days?" Henry Howard Brownell, author of
"War-Lyrics," answers the question in his inimitable poem, entitled "Abraham Lincoln," as with a prophet's vision, he beholds the "Eagle Armies,"
giving heed to the "*Forward, March!*"]

Tents on the Infinite Shore!
　　Flags in the azuline sky,
Sails on the seas once more!
　　To-day, in the heaven on high,
All under arms once more!

The troops are all in their lines,
　　The guidons flutter and play;
But every bayonet shines,
　　For all must march to-day.

What lofty pennons flaunt?
What mighty echoes haunt,
　　As of great guns, o'er the main?
　　Hark to the sound again —
The Congress is all a-taunt!
　　The Cumberland's manned again!

All the ships and their men
　　Are in line of battle to-day, —
All at quarters, as when
　　Their last roll thundered away, —
All at their guns, as then,
　　For the Fleet salutes to-day.

The armies have broken camp
　　On the vast and sunny plain,
　　The drums are rolling again;
With steady, measured tramp,
　　They're marching all again.

With alignment firm and solemn,
　　Once again they form

In mighty square and column,—
  But never for charge and storm.

The Old Flag they died under
  Floats above them on the shore,
And on the great ships yonder
  The ensigns dip once more—
And once again the thunder
  Of the thirty guns and four!

In solid platoons of steel,
  Under heaven's triumphal arch,
The long lines break and wheel—
  And the word is, " Forward, march!"

The Colors ripple o'erhead,
  The drums roll up to the sky,
And with martial time and tread
  The regiments all pass by—
The ranks of our faithful Dead,
  Meeting their President's eye.

With a soldier's quiet pride
  They smile o'er the perished pain,
  For their anguish was not vain—
For thee, O Father, we died!
  And we did not die in vain.

March on, your last brave mile!
  Salute him, Star and Lace,
Form round him, rank and file,
  And look on the kind, rough face;
But the quaint and homely smile
  Has a glory and a grace
It never had known erewhile—
  Never, in time and space.

Close round him, hearts of pride!
Press near him, side by side,—
  Our Father is not alone!
For the Holy Right ye died,
And Christ, the Crucified,
  Waits to welcome his own.

www.ingramcontent.com/pod-product-compliance
Lightning Source LLC
Chambersburg PA
CBHW020410030726
47496CB00007B/2391